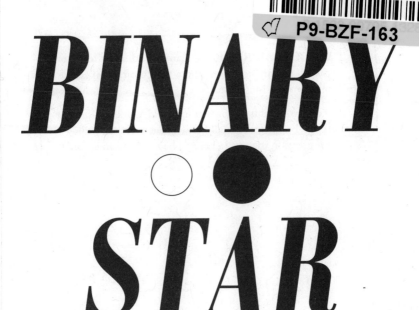

BINARY ○ ● STAR

a novel by ——————

SARAH GERARD

Two Dollar Radio
Books too loud to Ignore

TWO DOLLAR RADIO is a family-run outfit founded in 2005 with the mission to reaffirm the cultural and artistic spirit of the publishing industry.

We aim to do this by presenting bold works of literary merit, each book, individually and collectively, providing a sonic progression that we believe to be too loud to ignore.

Cover image by NASA/CXC/U.Leicester/U.London/R.Soria & K.Wu
Author photograph by Josh Wool

Printed in Canada.

TwoDollarRadio.com
twodollar@twodollarradio.com

Two Dollar Radio
Books too loud to Ignore

For David

"Down with a world in which the guarantee that we will not die of starvation has been purchased by the guarantee that we will die of boredom."

—Raoul Vaneigem, *The Revolution of Everyday Life*

BINARY STAR

I am a white dwarf.

I spend all my energy, compress my core, I ionize electrons.

Each night, I find the burning center of my hunger alone in my apartment. The walls breathe the space between them and the distance tastes metallic.

If I stare at John's painting on the wall, those walls left and right expand and cool.

Everything has a shimmer, including me, and I am empty. I find my emptiness in the center of the room: the dead space.

I and the dead space are most alike.

The sounds of Earth below reach me on the futon. I sit in a way complementary to my thighs: one crossed over the other, leaning more on the right hip than the left: a perfect balance.

There is work to be done, but I won't do it. I will curve around the empty space between the work and me, and we will fall toward each other but continue to orbit.

I will study the main-sequence chart on the wall, the one John gave me. That John's parents gave me.

The total mass of a star is the principal determinant of its fate.

A star is held together by its own gravity.

When I visited John in Chicago last spring, I awoke to his urine in the bed. He can't wake from the Seroquel he takes to fall asleep. It's pointless to try to make him. Even if I succeed, he's delusional.

That time, he was angry. He thought I'd spilled something.

What time is it? he asked. Late is not a time.

It's four in the morning. You wet the bed.

No I didn't.

It smells like urine. You peed the bed.

No I didn't. Snoring.

I blow smoke into the center.

I lie on the cold leather couch his parents bought him. Leather isn't vegan, John.

I didn't buy it. They did.

John is not responsible.

At two o'clock today, I ate half a bag of sunflower seeds and drank 20 ounces of coffee. At six o'clock, I had half of a raw carrot. I had a Red Bull at eight o'clock.

All morning, I tried to work the TV. John slept until four in the afternoon.

How many pills did you take?

What I was supposed to take. Two.

Whatever.

He has been alone for too long.

I don't have keys. I can't leave when you sleep this late.

So?

A revolution.

I can't be responsible for you.

> *Because what if you weren't okay? No, I don't blame you.*
> *Of course not. How could I blame you?*

We'll get used to this.

We'll find a balance.

Closer to you than you are to me. You are massive.

We need to do things on our own.

I can't.

I was alone in a second empty apartment with Dog.

To own a dog is cruel, John. To own a living thing is cruel. It's not vegan.

It takes time.

We only have so much time. It is only a matter of time until.

I do away with all of my possessions, including myself.

The scale in the bathroom sits partially on the bathmat. I move it to the hallway and set it on the wood for absolute accuracy. Zero. Give me zero. I was 92 yesterday.

91. One o'clock. Some of that is urine weight.

Soon, I will disappear into the wall.

Soon, I will be light as gas.

There is work to be done.

Think of class.

Tomorrow, I will go to the school where I intern.

My students will take in matter about stars. I will radiate it toward them.

They will expand and harden at the center.

Convect new matter.

They aren't not my students.

They're interred. I have to study.

It's late, I have to sleep.

I won't sleep. I never do.

To sleep is lazy. I feel guilty when I sleep. I don't need it like you do, John.

Just being awake burns calories. Just being awake brings me closer to you.

To perfection.

Tomorrow, I will work for free and then go to class where I take in stars.

A star's luminosity is determined by its mass. I am faint.

I feel faint.

I am reeling. I shine.

A binary star is a system containing two stars that orbit their common center of mass.

Binary stars are gravitationally bound.

Gravity is the way we fall together.

In personal time and in universal time.

Tonight is the end of all time.

Tonight I want to stop time.

My time, John. Your time.

John and I follow our paths into the center but we never reach the center. We are objects drawn to each other in space. We are space.

We fall together.

I am tired but awake. I eat nothing.

I eat nothing but time.

John is thousands of miles away but I feel him.

He doesn't call me.

Nobody calls me.

John calls me sometimes.

I try not to lie.

I just lied.

John loves me.

I take two Hydroxycut and sit on the red futon. I smoke and blow my smoke into the center and buzz. Sounds of Earth below reach me rolling like fog through the windows. I'm alone. I am always alone.

I'm disgusting.

Hunger burns and rises in the chest.

Up the ladder.

Tomorrow, I will lead a test on starlight.

1. Stars are born in clouds of gas and

       a. Thighs

       b. Arms

       c. Tummy

       d. Ass

Stars are born of gravitational collapse.

Stay away from the vodka, John.
One more.
Two less.
A hundred.
More.
A dense, hot core.

The total energy radiated by a star per unit time is its luminosity.
The more massive a star, the more luminous it is.
The brighter it burns.
High-mass stars rapidly exhaust their core supplies of energy.
And burn out.
I feel that this is the end of suffering.
I feel that I will be extinguished.

This is the end of indecision. Of two desires orbiting the empty space of why.

I will finally disappear. Be final.

Desire requires two bodies: This and that.

The final exam.

Evaluation.

John says: What does it mean to be primitive in the city? John thinks he's primitive and he thinks I'm primitive.

I'm indifferent, I think. I don't think much anymore.

I think I don't feel deeply for John.

I think John needs me. I feel this without feeling it.

That he needs me reminds me that I'm here, worth something.

I know I feel hungry.

Distant.

I feel dizzy when I stand.

I'm not living in a tree, John. No.

If you say so.

That sounds perfect.

I don't know what I believe.

You don't believe these things you're saying, either. You've just filled yourself with them.

You have filled yourself with me.

You don't even know me.

You don't even know me.

You don't grow your own food.

You don't grow anything but your gut.

I didn't mean that. I'm tired.

I'm lonely.
I'm hungry.
I'm sorry.
Self-hating.
Justifiably afraid.
Don't be angry.
Don't leave me. I'm alone.
I should be left alone.
I love you.
I feel this now as a kind of falling.
I just miss you, I say.
I need you, too.
(We pass each other and keep turning.)
John, lighten up. It's a joke. I said I'm sorry.
How committed are you, really? I doubt your commitment.
To what?
To the cause.
I do believe in causation. I believe in control. I control this, if
nothing else.
I control myself. You see it. It is visible in my absence.
And on paper.
In my performance.
You got straight A's? You do so much. Too much, really.
But those people online aren't your comrades.
If you can't touch them you can't know them. I know you're
lonely.
I don't like to be touched. I'm sorry.
Don't remind me that I'm here.
I feel one thing: afraid.
Guilty. Vile.
It's just that I miss you.
I'm sure that's it. I am angry at myself.
I'm just angry.
I am justifiably angry.

Fine, then I'm afraid.

I call him periodically throughout the night. I can't stargaze here. Otherwise, I'd be out.

There is too much light on Long Island.

He's up all night when he doesn't take his pills.

I'm sick. I know. I'm sick, too, John.

I'm sick of this. I'm sick of you suffering. I'm sick of suffering. I'm fading.

We know each other's sickness. It keeps us circling.

I ask him questions about it but he doesn't tell me much.

I also think he lies.

I lie.

How can I know? I can know very little.

I know he lies.

I don't know.

I don't know what he sees. He doesn't ask me about myself anymore.

I don't think he wants to know.

What to say? I am empty inside on purpose.

I have a purpose. I do.

It is making myself a star.

I'm serious.

I don't have a sense of humor.

I think it's enough that I'm morbidly interested.

It must seem like concern. It does concern me.

He takes his pills for fun. They're his. He needs them. He says that he doesn't.

What would your doctor think? Do you tell him?

Of course not. I take them, but not for fun.

Whatever.

We're different. We're also the same.

John doesn't know about my pills.

Once, he rear-ended someone on the Kennedy Expressway and spent three days in the hospital.

I couldn't be there. Should I have told him then? There is never a good time.

I didn't ask him, either.

Was this your fault? I know it was. I didn't have to ask.

He forgets.

He doesn't want to. He is stubborn. He overcompensates.

He has to love me.

We talk on the phone and he slurs his words, orbits nonsense.

What would happen if I left him?

Left him? I'm not there.

What would happen if I wasn't?

What would happen if I wasn't.

The work and me. But John is work.

I do John's work for him already.

I help John become me. It is the cruelest thing I do.

I am orbiting. I spin.

You can't drink with it, John.

I don't.

Whatever.

I read about stars. Miley Cyrus, Victoria Beckham, Lady Gaga, Princess Kate.

I buy magazines at Walgreens. Read the stories, read for class. If I have Adderall, I read all night, filling myself.

I empty myself.

I fill myself.

I empty myself.

I fill myself.

Again, I'm still empty.

My goal for the night: 85. Amazing!

I don't need to be full to purge. I'm never full.

I'm able to purge without feeling.

I'm sick.

Mass is a numerical measure of inertia and a fundamental measure of the matter in an object.

I take my picture in the mirror. I know how to turn myself. I want no part of my body touching any other part.

The mirror hovers on the wall of my bedroom. It cuts me at the knee.

I'm short. I have very short legs and a big ass. My thighs are thick.

Nicole Richie is long for her frame. The space between Nicole and her clothes is immense.

Beautiful.

They seem to orbit around her bones, her empty space.

She seems to be disappearing.

She is massive.

She has an impossible shadow between her thumb and her wrist when she holds a cup of coffee.

I covet that shadow.

I hate the shadows in here.

I am also nothing but shadow.

I take pictures of myself before the mirror.

I stand in elongating postures. I send them to John. Make him miss me.

What can improve? Always something.

Please tell me.

He doesn't answer.

I trim the sides of the photos. The space around a body. The space to the edge. I am nothing but a shadow one thousand miles away.

I am nothing but light's interruption by matter.

How are you feeling, John? Better?

I'm sorry I woke you.

A white dwarf is very hot when it is formed, but with no source of energy, will radiate away its heat and cool down.

A white dwarf is also called a degenerate dwarf.

I shiver when it's warm.

John's parents flew him here this past summer. John has never had a job. He is probably not capable.

For weeks, he sleeps on the red futon. For weeks, I walk the floor around him. The ashtray lies beside him on the mattress.

And the ashes, I rub into the red cover.

I blow smoke into the center.

John, what about your class?

It already started.

The one you were taking in the city?

I have opinions about class.

How do you feel about your class?

You take advantage.

You take advantage.

Your class is destroying you.

I destroy me. I burn myself away.

It would take me an hour and a half on the train.

You can't get it up.

What?

You can't get up in time to leave.

He isn't hungry. He isn't motivated. I am, but he doesn't know why.

John tried to tie me up.

He tried to tie me with nylon ropes but I don't have bedposts. He tried to tie me to the feet of the bed but the ropes weren't long enough. So he tied me to myself.

This is the only way I can do it.

I want you to hurt me. Please. I need it.

We don't need sex. I don't need sex.
If you touch me, I'll explode.
John tried it with knives and with handcuffs but he's a coward.
(We have the darkness between us.)
John tried it with ropes and cigarettes.
That's enough and it will never go away.
There's something between us that matters.
Degenerate matter.
That matter is darkness.

The degenerate state of matter occurs under extremely high density or at extremely low temperatures.

Its pressure forces atoms to shed electrons in the dwarf's core, which is mostly carbon and oxygen:

Diamonds.

The largest diamond in the universe lives at the center of a variable white dwarf star.

It is nicknamed after the Beatles song: "Lucy in the Sky With Diamonds."

John is very confused on the phone.
If I call too early in the morning or too late at night.
He is often angry with himself during the day.
I understand that I can't understand.
He is angry at himself and at others. He wants to do better.
Do you ever feel powerless? he says.
You must be joking.
I never joke. Do you ever arrive somewhere you don't remember going to?
I feel like I've never had a choice.
John is mad at his culture.
His culture has made him mad.
I am always somewhere without knowing why.
I want to know.
We have an understanding of damage, and of the fact that what is between us is only thought.
That I am damaged has a significant effect, it is very important.
That John doesn't know.
He doesn't need to worry about it. He shouldn't worry. He has enough to worry about.
It's my role to be supportive. That's why he loves me.
John loves me. He does.
Maybe he doesn't.
Maybe I don't.
Maybe he wants to hurt me.
Love is giving up yourself. He has nothing to give up.
John doesn't believe in sacrifice.

That nothing is substantial prevents him from owning it fully.
If I were perfect?
Nothing is perfect. What is a perfect star?
A white one.
They're all white.
No. Some are blue.
And some are red.

THE FIRST DREDGE-UP

A GIANT TURNS RED LATE IN ITS LIFE, WHEN IT exhausts the hydrogen fuel in its core.

Its surface is cool but its radius expands; it is luminous but has low mass.

The outer layers of the red giant are convective, bringing material exposed to nuclear burning to the surface for the first time.

This is the first dredge-up.

Last winter, we spent a month driving around the country's perimeter. John's parents paid for everything: hotels, food, and gas. Our job was to drive and come back in January: to find something new. At first, we didn't know what.

To step out of time, place ourselves entirely in the present, which is also eternity.

The week before we're set to leave, I spend the night at a friend's house on Jones Beach, cramming for a final. I call John at two in the morning, speeding on Adderall, and tell him that I weigh 98 pounds, which is true at the time. I had weighed myself several times during the night. Then I'd become afraid.

I tell him that I'm bulimic, which is also true, but not the whole truth.

You can't purge when we're away.

Then you can't drink, I say.

Okay.

We'll find equilibrium.

We make a pact for balance.

We'll shed our lives in order to see ourselves clearly.

As long as we're together, we'll be fine.

I agree.

This will bring us closer, I say.

I'm here for you, he says.

And I'm here for you.

We start in Chicago and drive west toward North Dakota. All of our necessities are behind us in the backseat. Two cups of coffee sit between us and two iPhones full of music, none of the songs repeated.

How long have you been doing it? John asks me.

Ever since I was little.

Why?

I don't know. Why do you need to drink?

I don't. I just like drinking.

Whatever.

Really.

Okay.

I never see more stars than I see driving along the edge of the buttes. We pull over so that I can see them still, and I lie down on the shoulder of the road to stare into the space between them. John stays in the car. The curve of the road is dangerous. John is often afraid, but he doesn't know it.

After a minute, he makes me get back in the car. He can't be alone.

We are inches away from the edge of the road and a plummet down the cliff.

I get in and shut the door. I strap into the car. It is dark like the vacuum of space.

I can't see my hands. As long as I'm in here, I'm safe.

We're silent with each other.

In the early days of space travel, researchers feared that astronauts would disassociate with Earth once they lost sight of it.

They would lose the sense of having a body that belonged on the ground, held by gravity.

They would lose their sense of human value.

Familial belonging.

And reimagine themselves as cosmic beings, bound by nothing.

They called it psychosis.

In July 1976, Russian cosmonaut Vitaly Zholobov suffered a nervous breakdown when his spaceship failed to dock at the Salyut 5 station and lost power for 90 minutes.

No light, no oxygen coming in, no communication with Earth.

They were on the dark side of the orbit. It was Zholobov's first flight.

He had to go home.

The next day, John and I do donuts in the lot of a Butte community theater. Leaving, we're pulled over and searched by a cop who doesn't believe that John needs his pills even though he has a prescription. As we wait for him to check our IDs, I read the billboard across the street over and over.

Hail to the Beef. Hail to the Beef. Hail to the Beef. Hail to the Beef.

The events are unrelated except that, if you take a wide enough view, they happen at the same time.

We don't plan to stop in Seattle, but John hears about a vegan donut shop on the outskirts, so he makes me take a detour, saying it's for me. The shop is flanked by a Dunkin' Donuts on one side and a Starbucks on the other, and is across the street from a Fantastic Sams in an otherwise residential neighborhood. John orders six donuts and four holes and we sit in the window eating them and taking pictures of each other and the display case. We finish and I throw up in the bathroom. I don't make noise because I know how to open my throat and purge in silence.

When I come back, John knows what I've been doing.

Going to the bathroom, I say.

Let me smell your breath.

I know that it smells like donuts because donuts are all I've eaten.

Show me your hands.

My hands are washed.

Eat another.

I'm full.

He's angry.

We came here for you. I'm not the vegan one here.

You promised.

(I lie.)

Later, I look at the pictures and notice a cup of Dunkin' Donuts coffee on a table in the background.

When I ask John to stop at Walgreens for Dramamine, I buy a bottle of Hydroxycut as well. I take them sitting alone on a toilet in a bathroom lined with stainless steel walls, like the inside of a spacecraft. I wash them down with water from the sink and hide the rest in the lining of my purse, so they don't rattle.

Most spacecraft don't have seats anymore because sitting is unnecessary without gravity.

Stand.

When I come out of the bathroom, John is at the cash registers buying a Mars bar. I read the racks of magazines and stare down the aisles of corn chips and candy and Christmas decorations, beauty products and toys and Ace bandages, and over-the-counter medicine. I relax my focus and they all look the same. I feel far away from everything.

We find a Days Inn and I stay awake all night staring at the parking lot, buzzing all over while John sleeps and I finger the edges of a *Star Magazine*. In the morning, he asks me what's wrong.

I couldn't sleep.

Why not?

I wasn't tired. Something was upsetting me.

Are you sick?

(Yes.) No. I don't know what it was.

Another thing the researchers feared was that, sending astronauts into space alone, they would lose the feeling of belonging to any species.

They would forget what it's like to be human.

We decide to use our tent for the first time in the woods outside Portland. That afternoon, we visit a small zine distributor run out of a ramshackle building set back from the road in a quiet part of town. We have a hard time finding it but John eventually recognizes it from a picture he finds online, on his phone. Closer to the road, there's a Chipotle on one side and a Moe's Southwest Grill on the other. Sometimes, signs are easy to miss if you don't know where to look for them.

In two rooms at the back of the otherwise empty unit, we find wooden boxes holding stapled-together multicolored booklets and racks of zines on natural birth control, the Zapatistas, Chomsky, bicycle culture, and primitivism. We pay in cash and John listens to the only employee talk about animal liberation for almost an hour while I continue to browse.

Big Ag.

Prisoners.

Sentient beings.

Violence.

Monsanto.

Mass extinction.

The guy convinces him to buy two more books, both about veganism, and a book by John Zerzan. He offers us bottles of The Abyss, a locally brewed imperial stout, from a cooler under the desk, and John accepts, explaining that it would be rude not to. I don't say anything, though I know John expects me to.

He and the bookseller drink the beers together, standing in the doorway.

On the way to the campsite, John stops at a convenience store and buys a six-pack of The Abyss, promising he'll only have two. It's the end of the day, and we're not going to drive anywhere. I need to relax, he says.

But you promised.

(I lie.) It's only two.

Don't be a drag. We're in the middle of nowhere.

We pitch the tent together and I walk into the woods, saying I want to be alone. John sits by the bank with the six-pack and takes his shoes off and puts his feet in the icy water, smoking. The day is cold, but the air is humid, and the sun is low and bright as I walk through the trees. I put my hands in my pockets and chew a stick of sugar-free Orbit and breathe deeply. I haven't eaten anything since this morning, but I don't feel hungry. I attribute it to the gum. The forest has a language of its own. At times, I stop chewing to listen.

When I return to the campsite, John is talking gibberish. This happens when he takes his pills and then drinks with them, or drinks and then takes his pills, getting ready to go to sleep.

Why did you take them now? I ask.

Everyone here is primitive, he says.

I sit down next to him on the bank. He hands me a beer.

There's nobody here, John.

Revolution is a spiral.

I don't really want this beer. I haven't eaten anything all day.

The people are ready for revolution.

His eyes are half open. He struggles to open them more, but succeeds in closing one.

Let's go to bed, I say.

There's too much to do.

I'm not sleeping by the river. It's getting dark. The animals will come out soon.

It's always night when the people are sleeping.

You're sleeping, I say.

No, I'm awake for the first time.

He thinks I'm primitive and I think he's primitive. We stay on the bank. I wonder how I can help him.

I open a beer and drink half of it staring into the blackening water. John opens the last one and drinks half of it.

The natives are sleeping, he says.

You're an animal.

You've kidnapped me here with the natives.

How many Seroquel did you take?

What and when?

Whenever. At one time.

This is not a democracy.

No, it's not. You're drunk. I want to go to bed.

Complete the circle.

I'm cold. Please come to bed with me.

I wonder if I'm angry. Do I feel it?

It isn't too late. There will always be revolution.

Until the rulers fall from orbit.

I light a cigarette. I blow smoke into the river. Ultra Light.

I don't want to go to sleep while you're sitting here in the cold.

He finishes the last beer and crawls toward the tent. I try to pull him inside by his hands, but he's too heavy. I sleep with him half-inside and the door unzipped.

This is like being in a tree house, he says.

The water in the walls is a presence in the room.

Memory may explain things, or else it may confuse things, which is enlightening.

Memory is curve, a misdirection, a reflection distorted.

I drink a glass of water and look in the mirror. I distort what I see.

The next morning, John apologizes for his behavior.

I see that he's embarrassed. I'm embarrassed. I look down into the river. Water rushes over a branch that's fallen from an overhanging tree.

I'm sorry, too, I say.

We agree that it never happened.

We agree to let time erase it.

We've been driving for hours in the wrong direction and neither of us has slept well. We stop at a BP in northern California and put two coffees in the console between us. We put the seats back and look at each other.

Did you know that astronauts sleep upright? I say.

I know. You've told me this before.

No beds. They don't even need pillows.

I know.

He turns on his back and closes his eyes, and crosses his hands on his chest.

Their rooms are even smaller than this car. Much smaller. Are you okay?

I'm just trying to sleep and it's freezing, he says.

I know. I'm cold, too.

You're always cold.

I don't know why.

Yes you do. You always shiver. You know exactly why.

I start the car and turn the heat on.

You're wasting fuel, he says.

Remember the time you gave me your coat at the movie theater?

No.

We'd just started dating. It was sweet. It smelled like you.

We saw *2001: A Space Odyssey* at midnight.

That night.

Then we met up with Michele at three in the morning and drank Johnnie Walker Red.

Yeah. It wasn't fun after that.

Are you kidding? That was awesome.

You haven't eaten for hours. How are you awake? How can you drive?

I'm always awake. I'm always driving toward something.

Right now, I'm driving a line toward the void.

There is work to be done, but I won't do it. I'll circle my apartment elliptically burning calories from the kitchen to the bathroom.

I'll eat a cup of grapes and purge, eat a cup of grapes and purge, eat and purge.

Fall into my hunger but never reach it.

Orbit its atmosphere.

Objects that fall into orbit around Earth can't stay there forever. They must come down sometime.

These objects experience gravity but acceleration cancels gravity. Therefore, they are weightless.

They orbit for months or years, but without periodic bursts of energy, they start to slip.

Falling to Earth, burning up on the way down.

We never see them hit the ground.

It's a month of orbiting the hole between us, of the lights of cities looking like land-bound stars as we approach from the distance. In San Francisco, I become viral in the upstairs bedroom of a Hostelling International and beg to be hospitalized.

Abnormal food behaviors affect the immune system.

I have made sure that John sees me eating. I only eat a little, and only when he's looking, and only sometimes. This is enough to give him a general impression.

Starvation causes cognitive instability.

It is not exactly lying. Nor is it purging.

John cares very little about a schedule usually. He is not aware of the time unless someone is wasting his. He feels that the San Francisco hospital wastes his time. Or he feels that I waste his time. Time is so personal.

John feels that his time has been wasted when someone leaves him. I'm afraid of this.

I'm afraid of being wasted.

I believe I'm a waste.

I have a fever of 104 degrees.

John lies with me in the bed and holds my waist and we turn together beneath the sheets. I burn him, sweat the virus into the bed, into his hands.

This is the hottest I've ever felt you, he says.

Fuck me right now and I'll burn your dick off.

Turn over. You're sweating.

You keep trying to be funny.

Turn over.

He sleeps in the chair beside me.

The nurse brings me food. No, thank you, I say. I'm not hungry. Or I'm vegan. I'll eat it later. Or I'm nauseous. I'm concerned about throwing it up and blocking my helmet's respirator. I get motion-sick, you see.

Just some water, please. My fever.

John watches me.

I'm angry.

I'm angry with you, I say.

Why with me?

You lied.

You're lying right now.

I sleep and feel the ocean around the city churn the sky and terrain together.

I like the attention the nurses give me.

I like them seeing the attention John gives me, especially because he's angry.

I like to make myself a victim.

I lie.

I like to be victimized.

I like when you hurt me. It reminds me that I'm here. I make you angry.

I lie in bed and feel the moon pulling the plates beneath us together.

I feel you move me.

I pull the sheets over my head and stare at the dark, I stare at nothing. I pant. I'm falling through space. I fall through a void without coordinates.

I think that John doesn't want to be here. I think he'd rather be moving. I wonder if I'm faking it.

I'm lying. Am I lying?

Faking it?

Am I being fair to John?

I wake with a tube in my arm. Calories.

I think I can stop when I want to.

I can be well when I want to.

I can stop this right now.

Be whatever I want to be.

Nothing.

Whatever I want.

What do I want?

Fill me with fluids.

Shed unnecessary matter, I say.

They're not listening.

What do I want without John?

I love you.

I want nothing. Nothing. I actually want Nothing.

But to chew on the hospital sheets.

A binary star is a system containing two stars that orbit their common center of mass.

The relative brightness of stars in a binary system is important. Glare from a bright star can make detecting a fainter companion difficult.

Except in the case of spectroscopic binaries, where we know that stars share a binary relationship by their shift from red to blue.

Stars will shift from red to blue to red as each moves toward us, then away.

In Oakland, we stay with an old friend who hasn't seen me in years. He's shocked when he opens the door. He comments on how much I've changed.

A complete one-eighty, he says.

More like a three-sixty, I say.

He puts his arms around me.

You're so tiny.

I've lost weight.

I guess I'll have to feed you. Bring your bags inside.

We come in and put our bags in his living room. John is upset by my friend's observation. I can see it in his face.

John, it's nice to finally meet you after… How long has it been?

A year last month, I say.

Congratulations! It must be hard to live so far apart.

Yes and no, I joke.

John looks at me, surprised.

We'd drive each other crazy being together all the time.

John doesn't find this funny.

Our friend invites us to sit and John asks if there's somewhere nearby where we can get a drink. There's nothing I can say to oppose this that won't embarrass him.

The bar down the street just reopened, says my friend. It's red and black inside. Hip.

We like hips, John says.

My friend is confused.

Sounds good, says my friend. Let's get a quick drink.

"Quick drink," John parrots.

On our way to the bar, my friend asks me if we've eaten dinner. I tell him not to worry, that we'll have something small when it's convenient.

Budweiser, Sam Adams, Coors, Corona, Bass, Grolsch, Modelo, Yuengling.

John and I flip through the jukebox playlist. My friend stands behind us. The options seem endless. The record spins.

Then it repeats.

What do you want? says John.

A love song.

Pussy.

I want love, I say.

You shouldn't have a hard time feeling it.

Burn.

That sounds like an accusation.

Okay. Motown.

Jackson Five.

No, Shirelles.

It's my money. He drops a quarter in the slot. Jackson Five.

You get three plays for fifty, says my friend.

Maybe stay out of it, pal.

Here's another quarter, man. He walks away.

John drops the quarter into the slot.

Jackson Five.

No fair!

Too late. He smiles.

I'm sitting down.

No, stand. Burn calories. It's what you want.

We hug the edge of the Earth all the way to L.A. We take turns choosing the music: John, me, John, me. We always end with John.

We play a game where I name a band and he names a band that ends with the last letter of my band. We play until we come around to bands we've named already.

We drive in circles whenever we leave the Pacific Coast Highway, not knowing where on Earth we are.

John reads to me from the books he bought in Portland.

All sentient beings have at least one right, he says.

He lights a cigarette and opens the window. Cold salt air rushes my face.

All sentient beings have the right not to be treated as property.

Do you ever feel like property? he says.

All the time.

Why?

You never feel like you sacrifice more than you gain when you go to the supermarket?

You never feel like you're part of a herd of cattle when you're sitting at a stoplight?

Yeah.

He ashes out the window and reads the page over silently.

Why are you vegan?

Health reasons.

Is it really healthier?

I don't answer. I don't know. He keeps reading.

I can't believe this stuff is true.

Like what?

Like, we eat over 7 billion chickens every year.

That's disgusting.

Male chicks are immediately ground up.

Ground up?

Alive. They're not useful.

Serve no purpose.

We drive a little farther and switch places at an Amoco. We continue to switch places each time we stop. We take turns navigating. When John drives, I read to him. He thinks that he bought the books in Portland for me, but I know he bought them for himself.

I don't care.

I feel they aren't real.

I tell him I'm too afraid to sleep while he's driving on the cliffs. Really, I couldn't sleep if I wanted to, I'm so awake. I swallow two Hydroxycut each time we stop, which is every few hours. I take myself to the bathroom before we eat and swallow more.

When I ask to stop at Walgreens for snacks, I get pills, magazines, bottled water.

He smokes impatiently. He calls from the car.

What's taking so long?

I'm in the bathroom.

You're throwing up.

I haven't eaten for hours.

Come back.

Coming.

The road curves.

A revolution.

Do you think I'm sexy?

What?

Do you want to pull off and have sex?

We're on a dangerous road.

Okay.

Maybe later, then.

Maybe later.

I look at my face in the mirror. It's full of craters.

Some stars are fixed and some are not. I am not fixed.

Some believe that our sun's companion is Nemesis, a red or brown dwarf, or an even darker presence several times the size of Jupiter.

Nemesis is not always detectible, but occasionally sends comets toward Earth and may be responsible for Earth's periodic mass extinctions.

Nemesis is therefore also called the Death Star.

It is amazing what one can endure.

I know each box intimately. I believe in the benefits of green tea. I believe that coffee is the best replacement for food and also the best supplement. I believe that I need its bitterness because I don't like it. I don't deserve to like what I take in.

Most things are bitter, anyway.

Most things harden when they reach my center. Are compressed.

Most things are things I shouldn't eat.

I pretend to like Tabasco because it burns.

I need to burn.

I am very scientific, or at least methodical.

Everything must be quantified.

I do constant research. I train myself to do it.

7 Diet Tricks That Really Work. The 25 Best Diet Tricks of All Time. Retro Diet Tricks That Work. 8 No-Effort Diet Tricks. Strange Diet Tips and Tricks. Wicked Little Diet Tricks. Cosmo's 5 Super-Simple Diet Tricks. Joy Bauer's 8 Clever Diet Tricks From Weight Loss Superstars. Diet Tricks the Pros Tell Their Friends. The Official Best No-Gimmicky Diet Tricks. 7 Stick-to-Your-Diet Tricks You've Never Heard Of. The 20 Best Diet Tricks of All Time. 10 Weird (And Sometimes Scary) Celebrity Diet Tricks. How to Use Weird Diet Tricks That Really Work. Model Diet Tricks. Simple Diet Tricks. 8 "Healthy" Diet Tricks That Don't Work — Prevention. Ex-Vogue Editor Exposes Models' Extreme Diet Tricks. The Best Diet Tricks (That Don't

Involve Dieting). Anorexic Diet Tricks. 15 Best Diet Tips Ever — WebMD. Dr. Oz's No-Diet Weight-Loss Tricks. 8 Diet Tricks That Don't Involve Dieting. Diet Tricks to Help You Live Longer. How to Use No-Carb Diet Tricks — 5 Steps. Models' Beauty and Diet Tricks. Expert Diet Tricks. Diet Simple: 195 Mental Tricks, Substitutions, Habits & Inspirations. 11 of the Best Diet Tricks for a Skinnier Honeymoon. Weight Loss Strategies — Diet Tricks — 7 Years Younger. Your Diet Tricks. Clever Diet Tricks From Big-Time "Losers." 5 Bizarre Weight-Loss Tricks That Work. Scary Celeb Diet Tricks You Should Avoid. Scary Celeb Diet Tricks No Woman Should Try. Jennifer Hudson Weight Watchers, Weight Loss. 4 Weird Diet Tricks That Work. How Kelly Osbourne Lost 70 Pounds: Her Diet and Workout Tricks. Victoria Beckham's Diet Tricks Revealed. Best Weight-Loss Diet Tricks, Tips for Successful Weight Loss. Fast Weight Loss Program. 5 Easy Diet Tricks to Stay Fit and Nourished. Getting Rid of Bubble Butts, Thunder Thighs, & Saddle Bags. 7 Diet Tricks for a Skinny, Not Scary, Interview. Diet Tricks and Traps, What to Avoid When Starting a Diet. Learning the Tips and Tricks to Make This Diet Your Last.

The Biggest Loser Diet Tricks.

Stars form in gravitational instability.

I want to go to the Grand Canyon.

I want to stand on the edge of its emptiness and feel small. Delicate.

No, fragile.

I want to sweat in the sun. Feel dry. Brittle.

Feel like mornings feel when I've been awake for days, because I'm standing on the dry desert earth, and I am part of it.

I want to stare across the desert and walk across it alone like the Mars of my mind.

If I wander far enough into the desert, I may become a dune.

And winds will blow across and reshape me, and I will see that my form has always been and will always be indefinite.

We're stuck in a traffic jam in New Mexico and I get out to build a snowman on the side of the freeway. Other people get out of their cars, too, and soon there's a small party sitting on the snow of the embankment watching the stilled vehicles extend for miles in both directions. I get back in the car.

I smoke the last of my cigarettes and John offers me one of his, and we wonder if it would be a good idea for me to walk down the onramp to the gas station and buy two more packs. People are honking but no one's moving. The brake lights of several cars ahead of us go off, as if their drivers have put the cars in park. The driver in the car ahead of us climbs onto his roof with a pair of binoculars.

John takes a banana out of the bag at my feet, peels it, and offers it to me.

No thanks.

I read the fitness spa billboard three car lengths ahead of us: Want to Get in Shape for the Office Party?

You haven't eaten anything today.

Yes I did. I ate some fruit at the continental breakfast.

No you didn't. I was there.

I did.

You didn't. I was there. I saw you.

I ate it on the way to the car. I was behind you.

He finishes the banana and tosses the peel out the window.

What does it feel like? he says.

What?

Starving.

I don't know. It's hard to describe if you're not doing it.

I'm just trying to talk to you.

And I'm just trying to talk to you about your drinking, but

you don't even think you have a problem, so where does that leave us?

What if I really don't have a problem?

I open the door.

Where are you going?

To get cigarettes.

We're going to start moving soon.

I don't think so.

Get back in the car. Get in.

I look down the length of cars and see brake lights flashing and going out for at least a mile.

It's the same as it was before.

I would just really rather you be here. I don't want to have to drive in circles by myself looking for you.

I get in the car and shut the door.

Just leave me alone, John.

Fine. You're alone.

It rains in Texas and we get stuck in the mud driving between cow pastures. It was my idea to stop and look at the cows, but John drove too far off the main road and slipped into a ditch. Our shoes and pants are full of mud. There is mud on our faces and on our hands. I think it's funny but John is too worried about his car to see the humor. I tell him he's cute.

We pitch a tent among patties and see above us a sky full of stars, all fixed.

All fixed.

John takes his Seroquel and falls asleep in the tent before I can stop him. I'm too hungry to sleep, and I lie next to him, staring up at the apex where the tent's two sides come together. An hour goes by in complete silence until I see lights shining through the flap. Four deer hunters hook their truck up to the back of John's car and pull it out. They offer me jerky.

No, thank you, I'm vegan.

Where's your man?

He's sleeping in the tent.

They laugh.

They disconnect the car from the tethers and sit on the hatch. Stickers on the truck advertise John Deere and a local radio station called "The Pig." They wipe the mud from their boots.

You look like you need some jerky.

Thank you.

That's not nice, Wade.

She knows I'm kidding.

What's vegan?

Still.

It's a dietary restriction.

More than that. It's a lifestyle.

I couldn't do it.

Tell you what.

No shit.

One of them spits on the ground.

I need a good steak every now then. What's your man like? He a sissy?

He's not vegan.

Is vegan why you're skinny?

Don't you miss a big rare piece of meat?

Not really. I don't like meat.

You're lying.

You're crazy.

Thank you.

No, I mean like, really crazy.

Thank you.

That night, I lie awake until the sun rises. When John wakes, he's upset that I left him alone while I talked to the deer hunters. They could have hurt me.

We make love in the tent and lie there to watch the sun rise, then drive into town for breakfast. I order fruit salad.

We go back to the hospital first thing the next day. I have pinkeye probably caused by cow dung. I throw out my contact lens and wear a patch over my eye. I refuse to leave the car because I think people will stare at me. I can only see in two dimensions and I can't see my whole periphery; I see ninety degrees to my right and that's all. I can't see John.

When I take the patch off my eye, all the world looks blue.

We drive toward New Orleans passing in and out of towns of clusters of three buildings, passing junk shops and farms laid fallow by the cold, billboards for Jesus and against homosexuals, for Popeyes and the American Bank of Texas but against Obama, for NASCAR and Keller Williams but against socialism. I eat four banana chips and regret it because they're cooked in coconut oil and sugar. I feel like a failure.

John buys us coffee with cream when we stop at a RaceTrac and I use it to wash down two Hydroxycut, then remind him that I don't eat dairy. My stomach turns circles in my chest and I roll down my window and stick my face into the wind.

John rolls the window back up. He's exhausted. His pills sometimes make him tired all day. I think he's mad at me.

I'm sorry we did that again, I say.

He's not listening.

I roll down my window. He rolls it back up.

It's cold, he says.

I'm claustrophobic. I need to move around. Or get out. I need some air.

Are you on something? You look terrible.

Thank you.

I'm serious. Did you take something?

What would I take?

Sit still. You're making me nervous.

I can't. My heart's beating really fast.

What's wrong with you?

I put my seat halfway back and shift around.

No offense, but you're kind of annoying me, he says. You need to calm down.

I am calm. I have a headache.

We drive in silence for a long time before John asks me to plug in his iPhone and pick a song. Brown farms flow past us on either side like muddy rivers. I launch his Pandora and scroll through preprogrammed lists of like artists. I pick Billy Bragg and choose John's favorite song. We listen for a few minutes until the station plays a Nissan commercial and then we switch to another station.

I hate that Pandora plays commercials, John says.

I guess they have to.

I'm sorry I can't drive.

It's fine. You're blind.

I really am.

You really are. You're totally blind.

We're silent for several minutes while I study the margin of the road. We pass billboard after billboard for the same strip club.

I need to go to the bathroom, I say.

Jesus Christ.

I tried to hold it. I can't hold it anymore.

I can't believe you sometimes.

Tonight I am only proud of my abbreviated parts.

I have taken in one half cup of Eden pumpkin seeds and one cup of coffee with two Green Tea Fat Burner supplements. I am thinking about the grapes in the freezer. They're little frozen spheres.

Cold food takes more energy to digest than warm food.

The body has to heat it up to break it down.

Time is a matter of scale and balance.

Equilibrium.

Of keeping myself intact while shedding outer layers.

I turn in circles before the mirror.

I urinate and return to the mirror.

I turn in circles.

I try on everything in my closet before the mirror and hate it.

I look terrible changing.

I weigh myself again and again and again and still I am 92.

By sunrise I will be 90.

When I die, I will be 0.

I walk back and forth from the futon to the scale to the spheres to the futon to the scale.

I urinate and drink more water.

I urinate.

You only see yourself, John says.

No, you only see yourself.

No, you only see yourself.

Every time it ends with you, John.

Tonight I feel the matter of emptiness.

I cannot control what my body does, though at times I feel I can control what I do to it, and thus what it becomes.

A morning is becoming.

I drink my Red Bull in the classroom this morning. I think nothing but feel my students watching me.

I luminesce. I cannot control them, I feel.

I cannot control the variable of morning. Of continuous morning.

This morning I was 92.

Still.

The longer I live in time, the less I believe in the future.

I am becoming in coming undone. I unbind.

I rise like the morning: revolution.

This morning, I turned in circles looking for my keys. I had never been asleep. I don't sleep anymore.

John suggested a unit on primitivism. I have become so much

him that who I am is empty. I have very few ideas of my own. I have very few new ideas because I am consumed by a singular idea.

I am an ideologue (an idealogue). I cannot teach them primitivism, John; I only teach the stars.

I have made myself empty of intention. My body is hollow: a form. A vessel.

An exploding vessel.

Gas.

To disagree with John would be to renounce what he believes are our beliefs, what I believe he believes are our beliefs. To disagree with him would be to admit that I've lied. He'll know I'm lying.

Lying about all of it.

All of what?

I believe very few things about myself. I believe in the possibility of perfection. I believe that I have mostly starved myself of will.

Something is dawning that I cannot explain, though I know it's related to darkness.

I am not really here though I am here, though I cannot be sure that I am anywhere, if I am even sure of that.

I mean that I'm not sure I'm anything.

Starvation is a matter of privilege.

I take advantage.

I stand at the back of the classroom, a core unhardened into flesh and reanimated, cold like space, and white.

I stand at the back until the bell.

I am always in the back.

This is how things are done.

This morning I turned in circles before the mirror so that I could see my back.

I know I am air because I hear and because I can see through myself. I would not if I was not.

Most of the time, when I think I have heard something, it is only my heartbeat. Sometimes it's so loud I can't sleep.

That's a lie.

At times I feel it struggle.

That's a lie.

I would not if I didn't have to. Do not if I don't have to. If I don't have, I don't have myself.

I drive straight lines across my back. My ribs, which are curves, are straight lines.

I have mixed feelings about curves.

These are not my students. They are only students of culture. Proximity does not imply a relationship. We are only near each other. We were born of civilization.

We hear each other.

We file out in a line that is rough at the edges and curves through a door, like sheep to the slaughter.

We moved in a clustered line down a hallway, some slower and some faster, like the river that winds through the bottom of the Grand Canyon. John disliked the canyon. It was just a hole in the ground.

Really a gash.

A wound.

Once, he tied me to the bed and played knives across my skin, but did not draw blood. John is a coward.

This is the only way I can do it.

Last night I touched my absence.

Beauty can be tricked into being where it is not.

It is naught.

It is not the past. Because the longer I live in time, the less I believe in the past.

I carry it with me but I can't carry much.

To consider.

We stand at the edge of the gash. We are there for a moment, but we see it. We see ourselves in it.

The river at the bottom reflects nothing back.

Is absent.

I found that it was absence. Only mine.

I am faint.

I'm often faint.

Our palms sweat together. The canyon yawns before us.

John takes his hand back.

He dries it on his pants.

He's dry and I'm impaired.

I'm hungry, he says.

This summer, when John was here, I weighed myself at least five times a day. Sometimes I am already in the bathroom. Other times I just need to have a precise number. We all gain weight around each other.

It is thought that our weight can fluctuate between two and four pounds a day, depending on a number of factors, including the proximity of one's companion.

And how much water one consumes.

In other words, how dry one is.

I have never liked water pills. I believe caffeine is enough. But still.

I'll try anything.

I drink four cups of coffee every day. The first, I get from Dunkin' Donuts. They know me. The rest, I get anywhere I can get them.

I find the displays in Dunkin' Donuts especially motivating.

I drink two 12 ounce Red Bulls every day, at least. Sugar free. Sometimes I spring for the 16 ounce can.

And tea. And water.

I make this a "thing I do," to always have some vessel with me, holding liquid.

All the time.

All time.

To train for zero gravity, I'd have to float in a swimming pool. This is not a real simulation, as water resists movement.

In zero gravity, my organs would drift under my ribcage, reducing my waist to a thin line.

In zero gravity, my hair would have body, lift off my skin.

My breasts would lift off. I wouldn't feel them.

Shed water.

And blood.

My body thinks it holds too much.

Which I do.

Some astronauts describe zero gravity as womblike: a more primitive state of being.

The human arm weighs nine pounds on average.

Not to have arms or legs or torso.

I don't want to stay in New Orleans, but John thinks it will be fun to go to a strip club. We park outside the French Quarter and walk through streets churning with bourbon and sweat.

There's a man dressed like Homer Simpson with an erection drinking beer on a barstool in the middle of the street. A black-and-neon devil flashes red and blue under a wrought-iron balcony in front of a tobacconist. Four overweight Midwesterners stand around an open-air barfront waiting for daiquiris to be poured from spinning dispensers. Old women in floral prints limp along with Big Gulps next to men with frozen margaritas.

Bars follow restaurants follow bars and music pours from every entrance, jazz and zydeco, and classic rock and Rihanna. *Yellow diamonds in the light / And we're standing side by side / As your shadow crosses mine.*

A girl in a string bikini dances in the doorway of a club painted red. She spreads out, holding the doorframe, and rubs herself catlike against John.

What brings you here?

Celestial navigation.

You're funny. Ten gets you in.

Together?

Separate.

John pays for us both and orders a Red Bull for me and a Dewar's for himself. We follow the leather curves of the club through legs pointing toward the edge of the stage, and sit at a table. Above us, a woman in a silver thong and tassels turns in circles around a pole in the shape of a star. John throws his Scotch back and watches her until he gets dizzy, then stands to order another.

You good? he says.

Not really.

What's wrong? This is fun.

I don't want to be here, John.

Just enjoy it. You never enjoy yourself.

He leaves me and moves toward the neon corner that marks the bar. The song changes to Britney Spears's "If You Seek Amy" and the dancer spins in tighter concentric circles around the pole. Then she stops, facing me.

She points her legs away from both sides in a perfect cross. Her skin is shining. She's radiant. Sexy.

She rotates slowly on her axis and slides down, crossing her ankles. She puts her hands on the stage, bent backward.

Mirrors surrounding the stage reflect her body from eight different angles. Every reflection is ideal, every line a smooth curve joining every other into a full form. She twists her feet to the ground and crawls toward me like a tiger, her hair covering her face.

Do you feel objectified? Disrespected?

No. Never.

Her eyelashes burst in black flames.

You have an accent. Where are you from?

I am here for winter from Russia.

Do you like it?

It's the same. Shallow, cheap.

The room spins and bodies move around us but we remain still. She brings her hands to my face. She touches my mouth.

You're beautiful, I say.

You like me?

How do I get it? How do I know when I've gotten it?

Do you see how she moves? John says.

He puts two Coronas on the table.

This is fun, isn't it? he says. Do you want a lap dance?

He pulls a fifty-dollar bill from his wallet and hands it to me. He's slurring his words. He's had drinks at the bar.

Are you drunk?

I am not.

You know we still have to drive tonight.

Yes.

I can't drive. I can't see, John.

And I thought you weren't drinking.

We're at a strip club.

You're a liar.

You're a liar.

I give him back his fifty and say that I'm going outside to smoke.

One more drink, he says. Then I swear we can go. Here, drink your Red Bull.

You can drive a little bit, if it makes you feel better.

It doesn't.

Bourbon Street is a hot mess.

I drive us past the Superdome and out of New Orleans and pull off I-10 just after Gulfport, Mississippi, seeing out of one eye. We stop at a Best Western that's full except for one room with two twin beds. It comes with a bible and a *TV Guide* in the bedside table, an assortment of Ghirardelli chocolates, and a refrigerator fully stocked with Coca Cola products marked up two hundred percent. The top drawer of the dresser has a guide to local restaurants that top out at P.F. Chang's.

John turns on the TV and falls asleep in his clothes on one of the beds. One foot remains resting on the floor. He begins snoring.

I turn off the TV and sit on the other bed and watch him. His mouth hangs open and a pool of drool is beginning to form in his lower lip. His tongue rests fat and pink over his teeth. A receding hairline makes a widow's peak above his broad white forehead, growing pasty with sweat. His cheekbones are lost beneath his cheeks.

I reach over and shake him.

John, you didn't take your pills.

Huh?

You didn't take your pills.

Oh.

His eyes drift halfway open and then close. I shake him.

John, you didn't take your pills. Wake up.

I'm awake.

You said you wouldn't drink.

He licks his lips, turns over onto his back, and brings his leg up onto the bed. His foot hangs over the side.

John. Wake up.

I don't really want to wake him.

John.

Snoring.

You didn't take your pills. You said you weren't drunk, so you need to take your pills.

I walk to the bathroom and turn on the light and look at myself in the mirror. I smell the tiny soaps and unwrap a plastic cup, fill it with water and sit on the toilet seat, listening to him snore.

I stand up again and get my purse and come back to the bathroom.

So, I'm out here alone.

I light a cigarette. I ash into the sink and look at the time. It's four thirty. The last thing I ate was a handful of almonds at eight o'clock, followed by two cups of coffee and a Red Bull.

I walk to the mini fridge and open it. Coca Cola. Diet Coke. Minute Maid Cranberry. Sprite. Barq's. Seagram's Ginger Ale.

John's snoring has become an oppressive presence.

I slam the bathroom door.

I blow smoke into the sink.

I turn on the shower as hot as it will go and undress in front of the mirror. I hear John's snoring above the rush of the water and imagine his tongue falling into the back of his throat.

The tops of my thighs almost touch. My lower stomach extends past my hipbones. My upper arms look flabby. I can't see my chest bones without pushing my shoulders forward. My collarbone looks okay but my breasts sag.

I turn.

My ass should have its own atmosphere.

I stand on my toes. My shoulders are too wide when they're seen from the back.

I turn to the side and suck in my stomach. I hold my breath.

I shouldn't have to do that. This is how I should look all the time without trying. I exhale. I watch my stomach expand.

I touch my hipbones and feel the hollow inside them and face the mirror.

I am so, so wide.

I'm fucking huge.

I grab the backs of my thighs and pull them apart, making a space between them.

This is how I want to look.

This is how I'm going to look.

This is 85 pounds or I'm fucking dead.

The mirror is getting foggy. I climb into the shower without feeling the water. It burns and my skin grows red instantly.

I hold my face beneath the full force of the pressure. I can't breathe. I lie down and close my eyes.

I hate you, John.

I stay there until I can't feel the heat anymore and a calm overtakes me. I breathe.

I turn the water off and stare at the ceiling.

He's still snoring.

I wait until the air gets cold.

Belief is brittle. My skin is dry and brittle and cracks. I am always bleeding, especially from the fingers. I do not believe that John loves me. There.

I believe that John used to love me.

I do without my body: I am you, I am me, I am you, I am me: I always end with you.

Do you remember what happened last night?

I don't.

The question is what do I want in my center? The question is What Do I Want? I blow smoke into myself.

Do I want anything without John?

I know what I don't want. I know some of what I don't want. I don't want to be heavy. I don't want to be a burden.

If I believe in anything: lightness.

I once thought you were a neutron star.

I thought I was a neutron star.

I could never be a neutron star.

There is not enough of me to be a neutron star.

A white dwarf is the final state of a star whose mass is too small to be a neutron star.

We're confusing terms.

A white dwarf no longer uses fusion.

It is held together by degeneracy pressure.

Extreme pressure.

This is the only thing supporting it against collapse.

This is also the only thing that keeps it from exploding.

A white dwarf depends only on density. A white dwarf isn't burning.

It isn't doing anything productive.

It doesn't matter that I'm not burning anymore. I haven't burned for a long time.

I approach my natural state of being. Cold is my natural state of being.

I grow dimmer every day.

Lightness very much depends on will. I have basically starved myself of will. Of want. Of whether and what I believe.

In happiness?

In being better?

Better.

I was born without will. I was born with certain beliefs.

In sacrifice. Humility.

I am mostly devoid of feelings on purpose.

Feeling is fleshy. Don't touch me.

If you touch me, you have to hurt me. I don't want you to be afraid.

What matters now that isn't?

You used to paint. Now, when you paint, it is shapes overlaying each other. Transparency. Reds, blues. I see through them all.

John is mostly concerned with appearances. In this way we're alike.

In this way we're destructive.

We have only ever believed in appearances. Even now.

You have only ever believed in appearances.

A white dwarf cannot exceed a certain mass. I reach a limit that my pressure can't sustain.

You want me to be better.

John wants me to be better.

John doesn't want me to be better. John doesn't want to be better.

John doesn't want me.

Is that true?

Let's stop. We're circling each other.

I feel that the sun is rising. I have made more coffee. It burns in the gut, in the kitchen.

I move from the couch. I am little but a shadow.

I feel that everything is a matter of because, because John and I talk on the phone but it is mostly trying to understand.

Now we're eating ourselves and the star chart moves and everything seems to be curving around what I want, but I can't find my way to it.

The main-sequence chart. Are we on the main sequence?

We're dim.

I'm the center of the room.

I'm fixed. I'm not fixed: I careen.

I've been still for too long.

What was I thinking?

I was thinking about the scroll. But scrolls end in circles.

Clothing tags. Toe tags. Taglines.

All seems to move except for me, and yet I feel that I'm in motion. I vibrate against you.

I'm spinning. I'm spinning. John, I'm spinning.

I'm spinning. I'm spinning.

I'm spinning. I collapse.

There are binary companions we never see.

Like black holes.

When a body crosses the event horizon surrounding a black hole, it shifts to red.

The body's redshift is its infinite gravitational lensing.

I walk down the street without feeling. I always move without feeling.

It is something I will.

So oblivion is a verb.

Redshift.

I think the pharmacist feels me. He anticipates my needs.

Can I help you?

No, you can't. I'm here again. You're in my periphery, so I see you.

You see me. You look concerned.

Are you sure I can't help you?

Actually, no.

The modern value of the limit of white dwarfs was first published in a paper:

"The Maximum Mass of Ideal White Dwarfs."

Can you explain that?

I stand in the diet aisle. Hydroxycut. Lipozene. alli. EAC. Metabolife. Sensa. ReNew. Natrol.

Zantrex-3. SlimQuick. QuickTrim. Mega-T. Slim FX. PhytoGeniX. Xenadrine. Dexatrim.

Thermonex. NitroVarin. Stacker. Labrada. Irwin Naturals Triple-Tea Fat Burner Softgels.

I stand at the counter. Christina Ricci. Nicole Richie. Portia de Rossi. Mary Kate and Ashley.

That'll be twenty.

Mischa Barton. Victoria Beckham. Bethenny Frankel. Allegra Versace.

Is that all?

Kelly Clarkson. Lily Allen. Keira Knightley. Ginger Spice.

Credit or debit.

Lindsay Lohan. Lady Gaga. Fiona Apple. Isabelle Caro, who's dead.

Felicity Huffman. Calista Flockhart. Tara Reid.

Karen Carpenter, who's dead.

Would you like a candy bar for a dollar?

Fuck you.

The Barbi Twins. Lara Flynn Boyle. Paula Abdul. Joan Rivers. Sharon Osbourne.

The ladder is the ribs, the lines in the chest.

The gap between the thighs.

I want the rings around the eyes.

Nobody ever talks about the giant black hole at the center of our galaxy, or the fact that most, if not all, galaxies orbit super-massive black holes.

It is not good for casual conversation to talk about circling oblivion.

Death.

By death I don't mean individual inevitable conclusion, but the death of any trace of any of this. Deep death, if you consider that death is a matter of time.

The nature of a supermassive black hole is such that the density of its singularity is less than that of a smaller black hole. In some cases, it is no denser than water.

This means that a body traveling toward the black hole center will not experience significant tidal force until very deep into the black hole.

An observer would notice very little change. Once a body crosses the event horizon, it redshifts, but it never disappears.

We stop in Savannah to see the moss on the trees.

We lie in the grass in one square, then another. We sleep with magazines over our faces.

John, I need to tell you something.

He's sleeping.

Can I hold your hand?

Why are you crying? he says.

Do you love me?

What do you want me to say?

That you do.

Okay. Of course I do.

John bought me this mirror for my birthday. Or John used his parents' money to buy me this mirror for my birthday. John used his parents' money to buy me a gift card. I used the gift card to buy this mirror for my birthday.

I look at myself for hours each day.

I see myself and in that sense I'm real.

I practice saying no to various kinds of food.

No, thank you. I've already eaten. I'm cleansing. I'm fasting. Making myself pure. Eating vegan. Eating raw.

No, thank you. I'm an activist. I'm starving in solidarity with Ethiopians.

No, thank you. Another time.

We go out to The Cheesecake Factory the night of my birthday. It's June. We drink wine and eat vegetables covered in butter.

John refuses to acknowledge the butter because he's been drinking since the afternoon. He says it is something else, but he won't say what. It doesn't matter. He doesn't want to see it.

It's not about personal purity.

But it's also about purity.

John, is it ethical for a vegan person to eat here, even if they're eating vegan food?

He's not listening.

I read somewhere that the Bistro Shrimp Pasta has over 3,000 calories, I say.

Huh.

I have taken too many laxatives before the meal. I nearly pass out in the bathroom and sit on the toilet with my head against the door, trying to see the tile. Everything is black.

My legs are weak. My heart is pounding.

John.

I vomit and feel better for having done it.

John, help me.

I try to stand and collapse.

I spend the rest of the meal drinking water. By the time we leave, John is talking in his sleep at the table. This is how he wins every time.

On the way home, I buy a bag of pretzels at Walgreens. I eat the whole bag while John is sleeping and then I throw it up. The bile gets stuck in my nose and burns. I swear I'll never eat again.

I lie to myself.

I walk away from the mirror. I look back.

I walk around in circles before the mirror.

The next day, John's face is slick and heavy in the morning light and he says that he doesn't want to drink anymore. I put my head on his chest and kiss his neck.

I'm so glad.

Oh, Jesus. Your breath smells horrible, he says.

I'm sorry.

It's worse than just normal morning breath. Go brush your teeth.

In the bathroom, I look up pictures of bulimia teeth on my phone.

It is raining in Savannah. All the gutters turn to streams.

John, I'm not starting a revolution tonight.

I'm not sure. Give me time. It's the only thing I eat.

I can't lean one way or the other. I lean in a circular motion.

Revolution is a pattern of return.

You want to return to where we started. So do I. I also want to run away.

A runaway star moves through space at an abnormally high velocity.

It breaks free of its orbit or else it's hurled free.

There's no resistance.

Moving away from its source, going somewhere, going any-where else.

Anywhere else, it doesn't even matter.

The red giant is inflated and tenuous.

We go golfing in Savannah with a friend we make sightsee-ing in the historic district. We had no direction, so we bought a Rough Guides and went where it told us to go.

Our friend is the son of a Savannah politician and invites us to his country club. The golf course undulates green into the distance. The day is bright and atmospheric and crisp. John hands me a Nike hat.

You need shadow on your skin. You're very pale.

I'm very cold. Aren't you?

We should have brought sunblock, he says.

Aren't you cold?

Not really. .

I ask our friend how far it is to each hole. He doesn't answer, but hands me a small white sphere with craters on its face.

You've got a tight lie.

Excuse me?

They haven't fed the grass. Your ball is close to the ground.

He shows me how to grip my club. I let him touch my hands but I don't want to lead off.

Then John can lead, he says.

John used to play golf with his parents, but he wouldn't tell our friend that. He didn't want to come; he thinks he's doing it for me, but I know we're doing this for him.

He's hung over. I know that, too. He swings.

Hit a skull.

I didn't mean to.

You're up second, says our friend.

While I'm teeing, he tells John about his father. I'm not

listening. I make a straight line from my hands to my goal. I lick my finger and hold it to the sky. My hands are dry and cracked.

What do you mean? says John.

They're disgusting. Half are crazy, half are drunk. None of them work.

Our economy is broken, says John. They have no choices. They're backed into a corner.

I turn to them.

An explosion. Earth everywhere. Backspin.

Nice one.

They're a bunch of worthless bums, says our friend. They're a waste.

Maybe they're not able to get jobs, says John.

Yeah, that's it.

I don't want a fucking job. You know what? I dropped out of business school.

That was dumb.

No, I had to. It was the only way I could live with myself.

Our friend snickers. Hope you enjoy welfare.

Fuck you.

Or maybe you have a trust fund? You and I aren't so different.

Keep talking. See what happens.

He's got a short fuse, doesn't he?

Don't talk to her.

I'm just kidding. Look, John: we're friends. He gets upset! I'm just kidding.

I'm not friends with fucking bigots.

Only drunks.

John, stop.

John's club meets our friend's ribcage. He falls to his knees.

Let's get the fuck out of here, John says. This guy's a prick.

You ruin everything. Why'd you do that?

The red giant is a late stage of stellar evolution, when nuclear fusion has exhausted the hydrogen in its core.

The core of the star turns degenerate.

The star expands.

The increase in size and brightness marks the beginning of the end.

John drives north from Savannah and stops on the side of the freeway. He hasn't said a word until now.

I have to pee. Pee now if you have to.

He turns on the hazards and I follow him down the embankment, past a sign advertising Subway, Church's, Quiznos, Taco Bell, and McDonald's, and one family-owned restaurant.

We enter the woods.

The trees hang low and barren and grey. The traffic dims to a hush. Dry leaves crackle beneath our shoes. We walk a distance and stop on either side of a fallen log.

This is where people get raped.

Turn around.

Don't look at me, either.

I'm not looking.

Don't look.

I squat against the cold bark of an oak and drop my head between my shoulders. I try to direct the stream of piss between my shoes but it splatters off the tree and I piss on my ankles.

Son of a bitch.

You piss on yourself?

A little.

John circles around to my side of the tree. He takes a clump of my hair in his hand.

What are you doing?

Fuck me against this tree, he says.

I just pissed on it.

So? He's smiling. So don't touch the piss.

He leans against me.

Stop it.

Drop your pants.

He kisses my neck.

Drop them.

I don't want to. We left the car up there. Stop.

He kisses me hard on the mouth. I hit my head on the wood and pain shoots through my neck. I slap him across the face.

I said don't touch me.

Fine. Be a bitch.

He walks away.

Haven't fucked me in I don't know how long. And you taste like shit.

I ask him to stop so that we can eat. He stops. I don't eat anything.

A binary star that is visual is rare. Its true separation is vast; its orbit measured in decades, centuries.

It moves slowly.

Did you see that asshole's face? What a pussy.

You shouldn't have hit him.

On our lunch break, I ride with my mentor to the supermarket. We both smoke cigarettes. I admire my arm out the window. The day is bright for fall on Long Island, and warm. I'm wearing an oversized Uniqlo sweater and a scarf with black Levi skinny jeans. For once, I feel good.

I noticed my students looking at me.

I didn't know you smoked.

I don't.

You're smoking.

I'm on fire. Just coffee.

No food?

I'm not hungry.

Or I have food at the school. Or I ate before I came. Or I never eat lunch. Or there's nothing vegan here. Or I'm feeling nauseous today.

You know what they say: starve a fever, feed a cold.

Are you sick?

Kind of, yeah.

I'll buy it. You look a little overworked.

We drive back toward the school with the windows up and the radio on the oldies station. My mentor sings along. Housewives jog on both sides of the turnpike in Lululemon activewear. Leaves dry up and curl into themselves, and fall from trees onto the sidewalk. Cars inch around the Burger King Drive-Thru.

So, any plans post-graduation?

"The next phase."

Exactly.

Not really.

That's not what he wants to hear. We finish the drive in silence and pull into the school parking lot. Students crouch low in their cars, not wanting to be seen skipping class, but we see them. He turns to me.

Your boyfriend lives in Chicago?

Yeah.

That must be hard.

I don't say anything.

If you ever need to talk…

Thank you.

I sit in different parts of the room. I imagine someone seeing me sit in different parts of the room. This person isn't John, but someone I imagine. Someone better than me. Someone luminous. A complete stranger.

This person is a woman. She is young. She is thin. She is sexually magnetic.

She has a lot of friends and she's the center of her social circle. She has a lot of clothes but she doesn't need to brag. She has men, only some of whom she pays attention to. They give her money.

All of her beautiful friends are as beautiful as her.

She lives in half-darkness. She hardly ever sees the light. She has her own light. She sleeps late in the day.

She goes to the beach.

She is constantly in motion but there's no separation between her movements. She is fluid.

She's white. She's so white, she's silver. She's glowing and reflective.

You can't take your eyes off her.

I imagine what she would think if she saw me in this chair. I wonder if she'd be jealous. She wouldn't tell me if she were. No, she has class.

I change positions. There. I lean back. I curve. I reach around myself.

If she saw me this way from a certain angle:

I take a picture with my iPhone.

From this angle: Take a picture.

Facebook. Instagram. Twitter. I wait for comments. Retweets. Shares.

I look for people to like me.

I look at other people. I look through a whole photo album of someone I used to know. She's lost weight. She's married.

She's happy.

She's successful.

She has money. Recognition.

I like a picture of hers and she likes one of mine.

I look through a whole album of John's ex-girlfriend's. She doesn't know I do this. I do this often. I take a minute to change my profile picture to a picture of John and I kissing deeply.

I imagine she notices.

Sickness is reciprocal.

Gravity is how we fall together.
If you're able to love, you can tell me what it means.
The way space-time curves around it:
Love is a black hole.
Undetectable except by the way it affects other bodies.
Invisible but strong. Inescapable.
You have a leather couch that I've slept on. You have a field;
I have a field.
If you stopped talking, you'd fall asleep, John.
(The red behind your eyes.)
I know that about you.

I sit in the back of the class. I haven't been to the last two
classes. My classmates know. They see how tired I am. I have a
24 ounce McDonald's coffee on my desk; it's mostly empty. This
morning, I ate half a McDonald's salad without dressing, cheese,
or croutons, and felt it for hours.
That's a lie. I have a very poor sense of time.
I can sleep with my eyes open.
Make your hand still. You're shaking. What does that say?
You're wobbling on your axis.
I can't sleep with my eyes open. Stop. Stop pretending.
Write this down.
(In your Mead notebook with your Pilot Precise V5 — the
only pen you use, because it makes the thinnest line.)
(What do they call you?)
– In 1860, Gustav Kirchhoff first put forth the idea of a
perfect black body.
I feel that I'm sinking but awake. My skin is dry like a morn-
ing after days of not sleeping. It is brittle and tired. It hurts when
I touch it. It bruises easily, red and blue, and clouds of black.

– It would be of infinitely small thickness and completely absorb all rays of any kind.

I feel my classmates looking at me. They wonder where I've been. They notice my unwashed hair. I haven't showered for days. I avoid the shower.

– We've since dispelled with the need for the body to be small.

     (– Or have we.)

– We preserve the requirement that it absorb anything. Anything.

– All incident radiation.

John calls me while I'm in class. I don't answer. He knows that I'm in class.

He doesn't know. He forgets. He overcompensates.

He wants to disturb me.

He needs me.

So I don't forget him.

What does he need?

What do you need?

Nothing. Call me after class. I'm going out.

Are you alone?

I'm with Michele.

Getting drinks?

My coffee isn't hot anymore. I pull a Red Bull out of my purse. I crack the can. It's warm. I rub my face.

Probably. Does it matter?

I thought you weren't drinking this week.

It's fine. I'm with Michele.

     This is what we do together.

It's what we do together.

This is what we do together.

I call him later but can't get him on the phone.

Charleston is a cluster of river veins flowing into the Atlantic.

We drive to the end of a thin peninsula and stare out over the estuaries. I wear a white cashmere sweater. John wears a red wool cardigan. We pass a bottle of Dewar's back and forth as the sun sets over the ocean.

How are you feeling? I ask him.

How are you feeling?

Really happy to be here with you.

This is nice.

It is thought that a white dwarf with a low enough surface temperature could harbor a habitable zone.

It is also thought that a white dwarf's cooling could draw planets in, completely consuming them.

It's raining. The streetlight shines through the drops on my windshield. They make a pattern of constellations. Two of them merge and slide in a stream down the glass, and break up at the wipers.

I blow smoke into the cabin.

I am at the center of an immense system. I keep the planets in orbit around me. I keep everything in balance.

I am a perfect daughter, student, girlfriend, woman. I'm admired.

I have roles. I'm a social human. I follow the rules.

I easily follow rules.

Men want me. Right? They'll want me more when I'm thinner. I'll be unstoppable.

Then, I will always be happy.

I open the door and step into the lot. Stop & Shop glows like a galaxy.

I'm a cosmic species.

There are no shadows in a supermarket. There is nowhere to

hide. You shouldn't be hiding things. I can only walk in circles. I walk around endlessly.

Every corner opens onto another aisle. Another curve. Another cluster of brands.

MorningStar. Capri Sun. Ocean Spray. Aunt Jemima. Quaker. Betty Crocker.

General Mills. Bisquick. Duncan Hines. Hungry Jack. Jiffy. Pepperidge Farm.

Mrs. Butterworth's. Campbell's. Kraft. Post. Hershey's. Carnation. Best Foods. Kellogg's.

Pillsbury. Nabisco. Heinz. Hellmann's. Hunt's. Frito-Lay. Keebler. Healthy Choice.

Kid Cuisine. Stouffer's. Green Giant. Ore-Ida. Smart Ones. PowerBar. Hormel. Chef Boyardee.

Lipton. Uncle Ben's. Rice-A-Roni. Pop Secret. Pringles. V8. Ragú. Prego. Tombstone.

I pick up a pepper, I put it back. I pick up an apple, I put it back. I pick up a bag of grapes. They're meaty inside. I find this disgusting, I put it back.

I read the labels closely. I calculate values. I bite my fingernails off. I touch my own skin. My hair. My lips are dry. I lick them. I calculate minute sums.

Everything is quantified.

I calculate time spent eating and not eating and what that will cost me in the end.

Is there a bathroom?

I stand before the meat. Blood pools in the edge of a pound of ribs. Bacon congeals in its own fat. Chicken feet cluster together under cellophane.

I walk through the frozen foods. I open a freezer and touch a box of Eggo; I touch a bag of Dole cherries.

The glass fogs. I stand in the center of the aisle. The space between the shelves and my body and the door yawns and is immense. I'm immense. I feel the cold of the air.

The fluorescent lights hum.

Go home now.

I pass the breads and come back and pass them again. Entenmann's. Lender's. Wonder Bread. Nature's Pride.

I pass the peanut butter and jelly. Skippy. Jif. Smucker's. Peter Pan.

There isn't a question of stopping at the dairy.

Sugar free fudge. Hot peppers. Toilet paper.

I find the bathroom and leave my empty basket by the door and stand before the mirror.

I am a complete slob fat pig cunt who deserves to be alone.

The sink is the kind that stays on for a minute and then shuts off. I push it several times and wet my face.

It's full of holes.

I find a pimple next to my nose and pop it. Pus on the mirror. I wipe it off with a paper towel and do this two more times for the pimples near my mouth and wet the towel and wet my face again.

My brow is dry and flaking.

My hands are shaking.

I start to cry.

I tear off two sheets of toilet paper and wet them and put them in my mouth. I chew and suck and continue to chew as I pick up my basket.

I walk back to the organic produce.

I throw away everything I've accreted.

I shed my outer layers.

I eat dark matter.

We don't have plans for Charleston. We haven't made plans all month. We drift from one side of each city to the other, in and out, leaving behind a trail of familiar signs: Chick fil-A, Cracker Barrel, Pizza Hut.

We find nothing authentic in the tour books, so we abandon them. They don't tell us where the real cities are. We look online and find the same information. We don't know what we're doing.

We drive in circles.

We stop in hostels trying to find a more rugged experience. They're just like motels.

How are you feeling, John?

I don't know what I feel.

The palms that line the streets of Charleston look down as we pass. We drive back toward the freeway.

We check into a room in a motel advertising heat, but the room is wet and freezing. I lie on the cigarette-smelling comforter and pull up my shirt and look at my hipbones. Razors. I feel happy, then I notice that my ass spreads underneath me. I pull my shirt down. I curl into a ball and touch my cheeks.

John spends so much time in the bathroom that I think he's trying to show me he's angry. When he comes out, he's calling his parents. I sit by the window. I smoke an Ultra Light. Not listening.

I stare at the palms that stand in a row at the edge of the lot. Skinny. Fronds bursting.

I take out a magazine. Ten Easy Tips to Grow Your Hair. Tricks to Make You Look Taller and Thinner. The Most Iconic Swimsuits Ever.

Look Your Best. Get Star Style.

Trends We Love. Trends We Hate. Perfect Pieces.

Secret to a Gorgeous Face: It's the Eyebrows!

Your mother called my parents. Do you want to call her?

No, I'll call her tomorrow.

When was the last time you talked?

A few weeks ago.

Do you not want to talk to her?

I just don't have anything to say.

I'm going for a walk.

Should I come?

No, stay.

I sit in a room of shadows.

Each night, I find the center of my hunger in the center of the floor, in the center of the room. The walls breathe the space between them and I am the space, condensed and expanded and condensed. I pulse. I've burned myself to cinders.

I feel that I and the sun are the same, shining on a side of the world where no one can see us. I am made of the matter of the sun, but I'm no longer burning. I've shed. I have little time remaining.

I pulse and see my structure.

I cool, and as I cool, I crystallize.

There is work to be done but I am work. I have goals. I am driving through space to reach them.

My goal for the night: 95. I drink ice water. I urinate, fill, empty, fill, empty, fill, empty.

It is about personal purity. It has to be.

Someday I'll be a perfect black body. I'll be perfectly smooth and white. I'll be obliterated.

Dark matter. Antimatter. Unseen, unfelt, unmatter. I unbind myself.

I don't matter. I am matter. I matter. I'm in the mirror.

If you touch me you have to hurt me, John. If you touch me, I'll be hard.

I want you to touch me.

Even if I don't want you.

I want you to hurt me. Make me absorb your radiation.

I am a diamond. I'm a diamond becoming myself.

Under pressure: the hardest.

Material.

That I will be the most valuable thing is predetermined.

I'll be perfectly clear and luminous.

I am hated. I'm a genius.

I'm perfectly smooth and white. I am rough. I'm full of craters.

I am one long line of everything you hate.

I am made of so many lies.

You see through me already.

I have curves. I have mixed feelings about curves.

I want to be perfectly straight and simple and complex.

I want you to want to touch me. I want you to worry about me. I want your attention. I want you to fill me. I'm empty.

I make you do it.

I make you bad.

I want you to empty me. Make me feel like nothing. Tell me I'm nothing. I feel nothing.

Project all your untamed desires onto me.

I'm a star that radiates but is dead. I've been dead for a long, long time.

Let me be the reason you're crazy. Let me love you.

Fall off your axis about me and my vacancy.

Show me how tortured you are.

We'll go around in circles finding out why.

I'm sorry.

I'm a sorry excuse for a woman.

Here's a list of things I care about: Givenchy. Hermès. Louis Vuitton. Prada.

I have never seen any of these things.

Jennifer Lopez. Donna Karan. Kristen Stewart. Demi Moore.

I have never seen any of these things.

Paparazzi. Scary Skinny. Açai berries.

I know nothing of any of these things.

I don't care.

I have never seen you open and flayed like a raw piece of meat, which would make us equal.

Let me see you. Let me see what you're made of.

You took us to a bar by the beach and all I did was panic.

We have nothing else to do here and it's been dark for hours in Charleston where boats trace delicate white lights through the water and the horizon line is lost in the deep black of night. The air is chill. I have taken too many Zantrex-3 and I buzz all over. I'm sweating.

I'm sorry.

My skin is numb and smooth and wet, like the mouths of the people around us. They eat peanuts, onion rings, jalapeño poppers, soft pretzels with cheese and melted garlic butter.

I hate that I'm material.

Are you sweating? John asks me.

Maybe, I can't feel my fingers.

You're hungry. Eat your salad.

The breeze from the ocean moves your hair and for a moment I think I love you and then I realize I don't know you.

I'm sick.

Maybe you've had enough to drink.

I rise and I sink.

Just sit down. Are you okay? You need to eat. Have some bread.

No, I'm not. I have to go. Where's the bathroom?

Inside.   ·

I'll be back.

John pushes my water toward me. I see his fingertips wet through the glass and I picture them on my face. The sight of his flesh makes me dizzy.

You're drunk.

You're drunk.

Yes, I'm drunk. But so are you.

You promised.

I lie.

Thank you for telling me.

He swallows the rest of his beer in a single swig and orders another. I watch the waitress look at him longer than she should. My heart is racing. My legs are weak.

I'm crying.

I feel like I can't breathe.

You're breathing right now.

I'm going to die.

Of course, but not now. You have time.

It's a matter of time.

That's right.

I feel that everyone is looking at me. They masticate their food. They think I'm funny. They're all as fat as I could be.

I'm ugly. Don't touch me.

I'm not.

Leave me alone.

I'm over here.

I have to leave.

Where are you going?

I'll sit in the car.

Just sit down, please. Relax.

I'm going to die.

You need to stop talking like that.

I stand. I kneel and vomit into my hands.

Jesus Christ.

Everyone sees me.

I'm having a heart attack.

No you're not. Is there a doctor? Anyone?

It's coming through my nose.

I know, I see it. Have some water.

I'm sorry.

Wipe your face. You need to eat.

I'll throw it up.

You'd better not throw it up.

I'm floating away.

I'm carrying you. Stop being dramatic.

Do you think I'm pretty?

You're fucked up, you know that?

Aren't you drunk?

I am drunk. Just shut up, please.

You put a rag on my face in the car. You give me water.

I don't know what's wrong with me.

Is this better?

Why are you drinking?

I'm not sure. Why aren't you eating?

I am.

No, you're not.

Yes I am.

John's breathing stops some nights and I have to move him. The Seroquel he takes to sleep makes him sleep too deeply to know that he's choking. I can only help him when we're together. When he's in Chicago, I'm useless. He stays out drinking late at night and takes the pills anyway.

Some nights I stay awake expecting he'll call me to say that he's dead.

Some nights I stay awake expecting to feel that he's died.

As if something connects us across the distance and he disconnects.

I cradle the sphere of his skull in my palm and lift it up. I turn it left and right, left and right, until it's perfect. This doesn't last.

Some nights I turn his whole body back and forth for hours. He breathes and then his throat relaxes, sputters, and stops, and breathing is a struggle.

The sound is so loud that it scares me. I've tried to sleep on the couch but I think that, if I don't go back and save him, I'll wake up alone.

I've told him to talk to his doctor. He's changed medications over and over. They all do this.

I've told him not to drink with them but I know that's ridiculous.

He snores so loudly sometimes that he wakes himself up and looks around like he's surprised. In the light from the neon sign next door, I can see that he's seeing visions. He looks at the backs of his eyes.

Sometimes I wake him on purpose and ask him to stop but this makes him angry.

That's if I can even wake him. Most nights I shake him and shake him and he never wakes up.

Or I shout his name directly at him many times, but even this doesn't work.

The day after one of these nights, he'll sleep until four in the afternoon. I spend the time that he's sleeping reading on the leather couch, or wasting away on the Internet, or playing with Dog.

I've never had keys to his apartment. He won't make them. I'm afraid that, if I lock myself out, he can't let me back in.

I've said this to him many times but he says that there's nothing he can do, that I'll have to get used to it.

I sit on the back porch for hours with Dog. By four o'clock, I feel like I've opened my skull and scraped the inside clean and filled it with dust.

I think that, if I can find the center of the noise, I might be able to make peace with it. That maybe, if it's the only thing I hear, I won't even hear it.

In order for this to be true, there would need to be no other sound. But there is Dog, and there is the fan, and there are the sounds of the building settling. Then there are neighbors.

I think that his neighbors downstairs must hear him.

They must have said something, if not to John, then at least to the landlord.

They are like watchdogs.

Do they lie awake worrying he's died when the sound stops

suddenly? Do they think about coming upstairs? About knocking on the door, to be sure he's still living?

Would they do that?

Or are they only concerned with their own sleep?

I've thought about calling John's parents but he would consider that crossing a line.

If John were to call my mother, I don't know what would happen. Something drastic, I think.

THE SECOND DREDGE-UP

THE RED GIANT HAS TWO SHELLS: ONE INNER, burning hydrogen, and outer, helium.

The star begins to cool and hydrogen burning is pushed to the core. The surface grows opaque. Convection extends inward.

The convective envelope penetrates the hydrogen, and dredges to the surface the products of the burning.

This is the second dredge-up.

I sleep a deep, hyperbolic sleep all the way to Raleigh. I awake with my face in the sun. It is wet with sweat. I'm nauseous. My mouth tastes like acid.

We're stopped outside a Shell gas station, and a thick brush forest behind the Shell. There's a picnic table between the forest and the curb, a few thousand feet from the freeway, where a family sits eating Lunchables and passing around Juicy Juice boxes.

The sounds of cars are a hush in the distance. A sign by the freeway tells us we can also find Cracker Barrel, Subway, and Quiznos at this exit, and a BP further on. John opens the driver-side door.

What do you need?

Aquafina, Red Bull, Ultra Lights.

Banana?

No. I'm nauseous.

I watch him enter the store and then I open the door and step into my Converse, leaving the laces untied. The day is cold and bright. I close my eyes and stand. Blood rushes from my head.

The hard air blends with the sweat on my skin. I'm alive. I have breath. I have heat from the car. I expand and I cool.

I sit on the curb and pull up my sleeves. My wrists are thin and pale and I turn them over, hold them away from my body. A semi-truck hauling milk passes another semi hauling bread. I place my hand before it and let it drive through my palm. The road curves. The truck follows it.

I feel that, starting here, I could become anything.

I feel that I could climb into any car in this lot. Go anywhere. Who would stop me? Not John.

Red Bull, he says. What are you looking at?

Nothing.

I got Corona. Let's sit at that table.

I'll follow you anywhere.

He seems to like this.

We call a Days Inn and reserve a room with a queen-sized bed and a flat-screen TV, which makes John happy. I use the bathroom in the gas station and smell the soap and rub it under my armpit and wipe it off on a rough hand towel because I don't feel like showering later at the motel. I don't feel like seeing myself naked.

We bring John's Corona to the picnic table and I sit across from him drinking my Red Bull and shivering, smoking an Ultra Light, which tastes like air. He slides a bottle into a paper bag, opens it, and offers it to me but I decline. Behind him, cars are turning on their headlights and exiting toward Virginia and South Carolina as the night falls, going wherever they've decided to go. Or at least, wherever the road leads them.

I think we should live together, says John.

I ash my cigarette. I don't know what to say.

You think so?

You're not excited.

I just didn't know you felt that way.

Don't you?

Of course.

John picks at the beer label.

It's hard being apart.

Of course. I miss you, too.

When we originally went to the moon, our total focus was going to the moon. We weren't thinking about looking back at Earth. But now that we've done it, that may well have been the most important reason we went.

The family that ate their dinner here earlier is exiting the gas station and walking toward their Honda Odyssey. They open the back hatch and pull out two overstuffed duffel bags. The kids each take one and walk them inside, with the parents following. Everyone is eating Fruit Roll-Ups.

There's a class I want to take in New York this summer. I can stay at your apartment and commute.

This is why. He doesn't want to love me.

What about Dog?

Michele.

All summer?

Michele would do anything for me.

I know this is a test.

So would I.

No I wouldn't.

I'm better.

None of these.

We look at each other for a long time. I wonder if he's talked to Michele today.

I know you would, too. That's why I'm telling you, he says.

Okay.

Okay.

So take the class.

You think so?

Of course.

You haven't asked me what it is.

What is it?

Vegan ethics. I'm going vegan.

The periodicity of Earth's mass extinctions is estimated at 27 million years, the same as Nemesis's orbit.

That summer, I take John to a party at a friend's house in Brooklyn. We get there in the rain and the streets are black and shimmering in the storefront lights. We hold our coats over our heads.

Inside, bodies heave together and the music is turned up so loudly it shakes the fixtures. Red Solo cups cover the floor. In the kitchen, a game of doubles beer pong has drawn a crowd. John looks around for the keg.

Where's your friend?

I don't know. I'll go and find him.

I haven't seen my friend since before I went to Chicago, halfway through the spring semester. I find him talking to a girl on the couch. They look happy. He is happy to see me.

When you have a minute, I want you to meet John, I say.

He's here?

He's here!

We walk around in circles and finally find John standing in a corner. He's holding a Solo cup and looking desultory.

This is the person whose corner you're standing in, John.

I hear you're taking a class in the city, says my friend.

Not anymore.

It's over?

No, the people who ran it are idiots.

My friend is speechless.

I'm sorry to hear that. What are you going to do now?

Nothing to do. Get drunk.

My friend looks at me.

You've come to the right place, I joke.

Good start, says my friend.

John holds up his cup and pretends to drink to my friend, then looks away. My friend looks back at the couch.

Well, it was nice to meet you, John. I've heard a lot about you.

Yeah, nice to meet you, John says.

My friend returns to his girl friend.

He's nice, isn't he?

He's okay. Kind of a tool.

I see a girl I know from a class and we fall into talking about deep time. John listens at first, but quickly grows bored and disappears into a room with some people. They shut the door.

A little while later, I see my friend talking to our other friend in the kitchen. They see me. I wave. My friend comes over.

You have to get your boyfriend out of here.

What happened?

He punched someone in the face.

He wouldn't do that.

Now he's in the backyard yelling with a two-by-four.

John?

No, our friend. John's laughing at him out the window.

I walk to the room where John disappeared. He's talking to someone on the street and slurring his words, and laughing.

What did the guy do? I ask my friend.

Look, I don't like your boyfriend. We can chill whenever you want, but not with him. To be honest, I don't know what you're doing with him. He's a prick.

He's really not.

He certainly seems that way.

John follows a few steps behind me toward the subway. I keep my eyes on the ground as it disappears behind my Converse.

That guy went down so fast. He screamed like a baby.

What did he do to you?

He was just talking shit, like the people at the Free School. Nobody knows what the fuck they're talking about. Nobody's willing to be militant. They're all a bunch of pussies who don't know what they believe.

You're wearing a leather belt.

I had this before I went vegan. It would be disrespectful to the cow if I threw it away.

Fair enough. But why is it okay to hit someone and not okay to hurt an animal?

Because that guy should know better. A monkey in a vivisection laboratory doesn't know better. He gets locked in a cage and abused, and he internalizes it, and then when someone comes to hurt him one day, he acts out and bites the hand that hurts him. That's understandable. That ape at the party deserves to get punched.

Maybe that guy has internalized his oppression, too.

That guy is not oppressed.

People don't like it when their beliefs are challenged, John. They're fragile enough already.

We walk past a dollar store and a discount clothing store and two bodegas. I stop to look closely at the ads.

I just didn't want to leave.

Are you serious? That party sucked. Those people are idiots.

He drinks the rest of his beer and tosses his cup in a trashcan, then asks me for a cigarette. I wonder if he's right about my friends being idiots.

What do you want to do now? he asks.

Go home.

Really? It's early.

I just don't feel like being out.

You're such a baby. You're just sad about having to leave the party.

I don't answer.

I don't know why you like those people.

I stand at the back of the classroom drinking mate because it's an appetite suppressant and has as much caffeine as coffee. At six in the morning, I drank eight ounces of rice milk with freeze-dried açai berry powder and followed it with a 24 ounce Starbucks Iced Americano. At ten o'clock, I ate a half-cup of grapes. Every two hours, I allow myself one half-stick of celery from the bag in my purse. At two o'clock, I can have one whole banana and my first sugar-free Red Bull, to burn it off. At five o'clock, I can have half a McDonald's side salad with no dressing, cheese, or croutons, and a cup of ice water. If the hunger becomes overwhelming, I chew a stick of Orbit. If, by eight o'clock, I'm feeling weaker than usual, I allow myself an apple after doing two sets of twenty sit-ups. Throughout the day, I take Zantrex-3 as needed. This afternoon, I will lead a lesson on common envelopes. A common envelope is a short-lived phase in the evolution of a binary star. It begins when a binary orbit decays or when one star expands rapidly. Write this down.

– The donor star will overflow its Roche lobe, initiating mass transfer onto its companion.

– The Roche lobe is a teardrop shaped region around both stars in which material is gravitationally bound to the stars.

– The apex of the teardrop points toward a binary star's companion. Let me demonstrate.

I tell my students to stand and we push their desks to the room's perimeter. They pair off and face their partners and join hands. Right hands hold right hands and left hands hold left hands, so hands are crossed between them. They start to spin.

Make a list of every way in which you're imperfect, I say.

Tell yourself that each item is correct.

Make a list of fears.

Tell yourself they're present.

Remember a childhood trauma.

Tell yourself it will happen again.

Think of your sexual inadequacies.

Tell yourself your partner notices them, too.

Think of your other inadequacies.

Tell yourself they're worse than you think.

Tell yourself you're ugly.

Tell yourself you're selfish.

Tell yourself you will never be good enough to have whatever you want most.

Tell yourself you don't deserve it.

Tell yourself you're not strong enough to act rightly.

Tell yourself you're fat and unlovable.

Tell yourself that the only way you will improve is through extreme discipline.

And self-punishment.

Tell yourself you're lucky to have your partner, as flawed as he is.

Tell yourself that these flaws are the very things that bind you.

They are the only things that keep you from falling down.

Because they are the only things keeping you together.

Tell yourself your partner is too good for you.

Squeeze your partner's hands until it hurts.

Get closer.

Spin faster.

Closer.

Faster.

Closer.

Faster.

Now spit on your partner.

I tell them to stop and look their partners in the eyes. I tell them to remember what it felt like just now when their partner spit on them, and to imagine that their partner is the only person who could ever do them that favor. They hug and turn in rapid circles until they're dizzy, then they fall to the floor.

When everyone is eating lunch, I eat my banana and then throw it up in the handicapped bathroom, then look at myself in the mirror.

I take a handful of water and rub it over my mouth and spit and wipe my face with a paper towel, turning my skin red.

I drink a Red Bull to mask the taste of the vomit and burn off whatever banana remains inside me. Then I chew a stick of Orbit.

Returning to the classroom, my mentor comments that I look ill, and tells me to leave for the day and rest.

I want to be envied.

I want to give out advice.

I want to have so many things to say, suddenly there is a book of them.

I want to look at the sky and understand.

I want to feel small.

But important.

Massive.

But beautiful.

I want men to think I'm beautiful. I want at least one to want to touch me as soon as he wakes. I want him to kiss my eyelids.

I want to have an affair that keeps me up at night.

I want it to leave secret marks on my arms and legs.

I want us only to see each other.

I want not to feel alone when I'm alone. I want other bodies in my apartment. They should be young and beautiful like me, so I can belong among them.

When someone is having a party, I want to be invited. I want to come late and bring beer, expensive beer like Space Barley, and I want every person at the party to be grateful.

I want that party to be held in my honor.

I want to want to see other people.

I want to enjoy a birthday.

My twenty-ninth birthday.

When I die, I want to have been on the covers of magazines like *Vogue* and *Esquire*. I want to have my own sex tape. I want there to be a star named after me.

I want to be Paris Hilton six years ago.

I want to have taken pictures with telescopes. I want someone to think I'm smart.

I want to want that all the time. I want not to forget I want that.

I want not to want what I think I want. I want not to want what I want.

I don't want to smoke.

I'm tired.

I want to sleep.

I'm afraid.

I want to be able to sleep in my car in a parking lot before class.

When I lie down, I want to feel something other than fear.

I want to intimidate people.

I want to go out to restaurants and order too much and drink Dom Pérignon and not feel sick with myself.

I want to say I've enjoyed something and really mean it, and I want that thing to be unconventional.

I want to be unique. I want to have thigh gap.

I want to see myself on television. I want other people to say they've seen me on television.

When I'm on television, I want my body to look damn good.

I want never to see a scale again.

I need to be protected.

I want to go whole days without looking in the mirror.

I want not to own a mirror.

I want to try on clothes at Macy's, and see myself in three mirrors at once, and look good from every angle.

I want to wear something and feel it against my skin and then forget that it's there.

I want to feel sexy.

I want to go to the beach.

I want to look good naked. I want to be in Playboy. I want a man to touch me without me asking him to.

I want to swim in a hotel pool, lie out by a hotel pool.

I want to climb into a Jacuzzi with other people and not stare at all of them.

I want them to stare at me.

I want to go back to North Dakota and lie in the middle of the road on top of a mountain.

I want to see all the stars at once.

I want someone to see me doing it. I also want to be alone. I'm never alone.

I want someone I don't know to tell me I'm pretty.

And I want to believe them.

I want to get fan mail.

I want to tell people what brand of clothes I'm wearing.

When I do something well, I want to know it before someone tells me. When they tell me, I want to feel proud.

I want to feel anything deeply.

I want to know what I'm feeling.

Then I want to be coy and not tell people about it.

I want them to ask. I want them to insist.

I want to feel like I've done something useful today.

Like I should go home and rest and wake up in the morning. Feeling refreshed.

I want to wake at a reasonable hour and feel okay with that.

I want to see the sunrise after walking around a city all night.

I want to take a shower without seeing myself from the doorway.

Without having to look down.

I want to look forward.

Into the camera.

I want my selfies to get a thousand likes each.

I want to be in an Herbal Essences commercial.

I want to take a shower with a man, and I want us to clean each other, and I want it to be sweet, and I want to lie in bed afterward still wet, and for us to fall asleep together.

I want my vagina to get wet.

I want to have my period.

I want to talk about my period with other women.

I want to complain to other women about men not leaving me alone.

I want to be fed.

I want to taste something. I want to enjoy the taste.

Of anything.

I want to make foods my mother fed me.

I want to make her proud.

I want to be there when she dies.

I'm so afraid that she might die.

I want to hold her hand because there's something strong and comforting in it.

Help me, Mom.

When I die, I want my children to be there.

I want to grow old and watch them grow older, and feel proud. I want them to be like me, but better.

I want to look at their father and have an understanding about our family.

I want to take them traveling with me when I leave the country on business.

I want to leave the country.

I want to leave.

The crystal structure at the core of a white dwarf is a body-centered cubic lattice.

The space between us grows smaller.

In a dark apartment, I walk the hallway dividing the kitchen from the bathroom. I talk to you.

A stack of *Star Magazines* sags on the table; a stack of *InTouch Weekly* molds by the toilet. Between them, a balance.

I'm hardening in the center.

You're what?

Becoming more myself.

That's good.

What about you?

I lie on the floor and compress my torso. I take handfuls of flesh and twist. I pull them away. I show my body what it is to dispose of itself. To get to the core. To release.

I wish you could see me right now, without a body.

You have done with your day. You have burned yourself away.

I wish.

What will you do when the river rises?

I'll do nothing, you say. I'll hammer it back together.

Sure you will. What can you do?

You have fantasies about a manifesto. You read me pages and words move about on the page. You're asleep.

We, Students for Liberation, call for a revolution.

You return to them over and over. My opinion?

Burn them, John. They mean nothing.

You have ideas for the revolution: *All governments and organizations that aid or support the illegitimate terrorist state.*

We'll live in the forest, you say.

Bullshit. You can't live without Pandora.

Forage? Eat animals when you hunt them. Make a circle.

I am an animal. You're an animal.

We, your Sons and Daughters, are calling for an end.

You're behaving like an animal. You're behaving like my animal.

You're mine. You're my anti-terrorist terrorist animal.

What will you do when you have to? Burn it.

What are my plans post-graduation? Stand at the precipice looking down.

I leave scars on my stomach. I beat them. I bite them and spit. I burn them. I feel nothing.

I chew, I spit, I chew, I spit, I chew, I spit, I chew until my gums bleed black. I chew my tongue front to back. I'm raw.

We want the world to know the real terrorists.

The main-sequence chart is coming off the wall. It obstructs the light in a triangle. Chew it off.

I rub ash into the cover. Chew something, anything.

Are you awake? Read it over. I didn't catch the last part, John. Read it over and over again. Read it over and over and over. The red giant star is a red futon cover is a cover is a roof.

Dedication to use all our means.

How big will the tree house be? Will it really be a tree? Will we have running water?

Don't be selfish.

Say you love me.

We are fighting to bring liberation to our comrades.

Say you miss me. Please just say it.

I do.

I do.

I know you do.

It's hot but we've been inside all day and the sun is beginning to set on Long Island. We walk to the ABC Liquors and John argues with the man behind the counter because we both forgot our IDs and I look barely fifteen. The man knows us and is only giving John a hard time because John is wearing a VEGAN shirt and seems to invite conflict with it everywhere he goes, which is the point. They argue about the sanctity or not of veganism for several minutes before the issue of the ID comes up and John calls the man an animal killer, and throws a twenty-dollar bill at him. Then we leave.

The roofs of squat, grey strip malls form a jagged line following the turnpike stoplight after stoplight into the impending dark. I sense that John has forgotten the liquor store clerk already.

You know we can't go back there, I say.

Why not?

Because you offended him.

Do you care?

It's the only place within walking distance.

If you really care, then drive to another place.

Seems to me that would burn gas unnecessarily.

I think about saying more but I don't. John finds me tiresome. He is also bored here.

I stop at the Walgreens and say that I'll just be a minute, and John smokes a cigarette outside by the automatic doors. When I come out with a bag of magazines, he takes them from me and throws them into a trashcan.

What the fuck?

What do you like about those things?

I don't know. I like the stories.

They're for dimwits.

No, they're not.

He looks at me for a long time.

I don't want you reading them anymore. They're brainwashing you. Do you like being brainwashed?

I walk around him and pull the bag out of the trashcan with the magazines still inside. I start across the lot and John follows behind me. At the edge of the sidewalk, he catches up with me.

You're mad.

It's not funny.

I'm not trying to be funny.

He pushes me down on the grass.

Why did you do that?

You toppled over.

Why would you do that?

I didn't. You did.

Cut it out.

I stand up and walk away. He does it again.

What are you doing?

You keep falling over.

He does it again.

Seriously, stop.

Stop falling.

He does it again and I stay on the grass this time. I look around at the manicured lawns and the single-family homes looking back at me. Across the street, a couple leaves an electronics store carrying a Sony HD-TV and plastic bags full of smaller items. Cars inch around Dairy Queen. I pull up my knees and get comfortable.

Are you just going to stay there?

If I stand up, you'll do it again.

That's right.

So, why would I stand up?

Because otherwise, you just have to sit there on the grass like a little bitch. He's smiling.

We stare at each other for several seconds. Finally, I take out a magazine and start to read. Demi Moore on Her 20-Pound Weight Loss. Skinny Jeans! How Stars Get Skinny in Time for Summer. Cameron's Red Carpet Confession: "I Didn't Eat All Day!"

You know I have the keys to the apartment, I say.

Best and Worst Beach Bodies. Stars With Cellulite. Best Butts.

If you want to drink that beer, I have to let you in.

You really don't get it, he says.

You can't drink that Corona on the sidewalk. I get that.

You're really sick.

I look at him.

I won't do it again, he says.

He holds out his hand and I take it.

Fuck you, I say.

Fuck you, too, he says.

You know, you're sick, too.

That night, we watch a documentary about the Earth Liberation Front. We see the charred remains of the offices of Superior Lumber, keyboards melted together and aluminum chairs twisted around themselves like wrought skeletons.

I thought the ELF was nonviolent, I say.

They are.

But this is arson.

Who was injured?

Mom, it's me. We're in Baltimore.

I'm sorry. I thought you'd be mad, which you are.

Yeah, we're having fun.

I'm just not feeling well.

You know how I get in the car.

It's not the flu. It's motion sickness.

I haven't been able to eat very much.

We're having a good time.

Just mostly motels.

Not tonight. We're staying with Helen.

I'll tell her you said so.

I'm fine.

I'll have John stop somewhere.

I'll tell him you said hello.

Hey, Mom? Can I tell you something?

Never mind.

No, nothing. How are you?

It's just that… well, I've been sad.

I don't know.

I think I'm overwhelmed. I don't know with what.

I'm sure it's nothing. I'll be fine.

I don't think I need to see anyone about it.

St. John's Wort. Okay.

I will. Thank you.

I love you, too.

In Baltimore, we stay with a friend of my mother. She's pre-pared a crab feast without knowing that we're vegan. The last time she saw me, I was twelve and we made crab cakes from scratch. She remembers how much I loved them.

By the time we arrive, at dusk, everyone is waiting. She's invited six or seven other people my mother's age, who talk to John and me with the kind of intentional respect older people give to young adults. They ask me what I'm studying.

Astronomy. Education.

Am I going to be an astronaut?

Space scares me.

They find this funny. We stand around in the kitchen. A box of roasted crabs sits, closed, on a table covered with paper. '90s music plays on a small Sony stereo. Our host hands us two Bud Lights.

You're old enough to drink them now! she says. Last time I saw you, you were…

She holds up her hand to her breast.

It's been a long time, I say.

It's been too long. I've got more past than future now. Lord! Don't ever get old.

I would never.

She opens the box and turns it upside-down. Red bodies spill across the butcher paper and the smell of Old Bay fills the tiny bare-wood kitchen. Star shapes crisscross each other limply and her friends begin tearing shells apart with their hands. John and I stand in the doorway.

What's wrong? she asks us.

To be honest: we're vegan.

Oh, no!

We should have told you.

I didn't realize! I just want to make sure you're fed.

She opens the refrigerator and bends down to search inside. John and I look at each other. We know what's coming.

Potato salad?

No, sorry. It's not vegan.

Leftover spaghetti?

What kind of sauce?

Vodka.

No, sorry.

Nutella and jelly?

John touches my shoulder.

You know, we can just go out and grab something, I say. It might be easier. We won't be gone very long.

Don't do that. I'd feel too bad.

It's okay. This happens all the time.

Do you both have to go?

I look at John. He wouldn't want to be alone if I stayed here.

We'll both go. Be right back.

Don't tell your mother.

I don't tell her anything.

She laughs.

Mass transfer in a binary system shrinks the orbit, causing an accelerated overflow of the donor star's Roche lobe.

This initiates a runaway process of mass transfer that engulfs the star's companion in a common envelope.

Shrinking ends when the envelope is expelled or when the two stars merge and no more energy is available either to expand or expel the envelope.

This is called the spiral-in.

That night, we sleep on an air mattress our host lays out on the floor of the living room. It fills the area between the couch and the front windows and from the front door to the TV: almost the whole space. When I get up to go to the bathroom in the middle of the night, I walk on air. I come back and walk on air and lie down next to John. I put my arm around his stomach.

When we first started dating, we camped by the Long Island Sound with two friends I've since fallen out with. We drank around the fire and made sandwiches with Nestlé graham crackers and Hershey's bars, and marshmallows they stabbed with the ends of sticks and held to the edge of the flames. We talked until the sun began to rise, then we put out the fire and retired to our North Face tents and John shared mine. I slept with my arm around him, just like this, and felt his chest rise and fall. It was our first time sleeping together.

That afternoon, I woke with a spider bite on my neck and he kissed it. We made love in the tent and the time outside didn't matter. It didn't even exist.

John rolls over and kisses me on the forehead and we lie with our arms around each other for a long time. My face is pressed against his chest. I breathe in his smell. I kiss his collarbone.

He runs his fingers around the elastic waistband of my shorts and pushes it down, then he pushes me onto my back. He climbs on top of me and pulls my shorts down to my ankles, and I feel his dick grow hard against me.

I lick my fingers and wet myself. I take him in my hand. He pushes inside me.

Bursts of color appear behind my eyes. Sharp pain shoots through my abdomen. My breath catches. I stretch around him. He grows harder inside me and thrusts. I lick my fingers again.

I'm dry. John moves slowly.

Is this hurting you?

A little, but it's okay.

I don't want to hurt you.

No, it feels good.

Kiss me.

He buries his head in my shoulder. His movements are slow and rhythmic. I feel him coming deep inside me.

Afterward, he lies next to me, our sweat cooling.

That was really good.

Yeah.

I love you, he says.

I know you do.

Did you come?

Yes.

Really?

No.

But sometimes it's hard for me.

I just want you to feel good.

I do.

Okay.

He touches between my legs.

You're not just saying that?

Why would I lie about it?

The next day, the arteries leading into New York are clogged. We sit in an hours-long traffic jam, during which it begins to snow. In the sky above the billboards for Manhattan Mini Storage, Kars4Kids, and GEICO, white and grey clouds recess into themselves in soft folding shapes. We play a game where we try to say the same word at the same time without any clues.

Last night, I washed down 20 milligrams of Adderall with two Red Bulls. At seven o'clock this morning, I ate two Hydroxycuts and dressed for class. On the way there, I ate an apple and drank 24 ounces of coffee. I'm sitting in the front row because this is where I was told to sit. I can't feel my body in my chair. The fluorescent lights buzz against the walls, which seem to be full of water. My professor makes eye contact with me when I first arrive, but then doesn't look at me for the rest of the class. I take twenty pages of notes in two hours. I count them. I write neatly, as small as I can, but my hand shakes and sometimes I lose control of the line.

– The white dwarf is supported against collapse by degeneracy pressure.

John texts me.

Second draft of the manifesto.

I'm in class.

– The temperature rises within a white dwarf accreting matter from its companion.

  – It doesn't expand and cool.

I'll send it to you now. Read it when you can.

I will.

– The star increases in temperature, not in pressure.

You're in, aren't you?

Of course. I want to help.

– Carbon fusion in the core reignites — runaway process that feeds on itself.

As I'm leaving, my professor pulls me aside.

You slipped a little on the last test.

I know. I didn't have time to study.

I realize I'm grinding my jaw and stop. My forehead tenses. I relax it.

Well, get the notes from someone next time.

I will.

You only have one more absence this semester.

I won't miss any more class.

He smiles. He's about to make a joke.

And don't sit in the back. It's like you're hiding something.

To be honest, I have a thyroid condition. It was just diagnosed. That's why I've missed classes.

I've said too much already.

So, if you notice me losing weight, you'll know that's why.

He looks at me for a long time. He knows I'm lying.

I haven't noticed, yet, but I'll keep that in mind. I'm sorry about your condition.

It's under control.

We remain standing mutely in the doorway.

If you ever need to see me, you know where to find me.

Thank you.

My downstairs neighbor's dog barks until five in the morning the night we return to New York. John plans to leave at eight to drive back to Chicago. He takes his Seroquel at midnight and asks me to wake him at seven to say a proper goodbye. I'm awake for most of the night. I'm awake when my alarm goes off. He's sluggish and falls asleep on the red futon while I'm in the bathroom. I make coffee and try to convince him to sleep more, but he still drives away. I watch from the sidewalk and feel a profound absence.

He doesn't call from the road and when I call him, he doesn't answer. I call twenty times. I email. I text. I call Michele.

Have you seen John?

She hasn't.

He should have been back tonight.

He'll call you when he's back, I'm sure.

I picture him driving around in circles. He's lost.

I picture him overturned in a ditch.

The next morning, he calls to say he's sorry, that he pulled off in Ohio and woke up ten hours later in his car.

I was in the middle of nowhere. So many stars. Like driving through North Dakota.

I told you to stay here and sleep.

I'm home now.

I thought you were dead.

Don't be dramatic.

That night, he gets drunk by himself and falls asleep in the bushes outside his apartment. His neighbor wakes him at six in the morning, when he goes out to get his newspaper. John has cuts and bruises on his face that he doesn't remember getting in a fight, though the patterns suggest someone hit him very hard. I tell him to go to the hospital and get x-rayed, but he thinks it's unnecessary.

Michele thinks he's fine.

You have an atmosphere. I have an atmosphere.

You stand on one side of the bed and I stand on the other and you tell me what you think of my clothing. You leave Dog in the crate all day while you sleep. She has to pee. She's an animal, John.

Say you can't help it, but maybe consider you own her.

Mornings feel like paper.

A morning is continuous. You don't realize it if you sleep when it's dark. You wake suddenly in the light and there is division between one time and another.

I tell you now: There's no division. You have more past than future? No, you don't. You have neither.

You have only the present.

It is cruel to own an animal: not vegan.

I stand at the foot of your bed and talk like a child. I pulse against the cock you can't use.

You treat me like a dog.

This is the only way you can do it. This is the only way you will do it.

That was the best sex we've ever had and you thought it was an insult.

It pays to be unspecific.

It's true that I miss you. It's true that I wish you were here. I follow you endlessly reaching and never reach you. You follow behind me.

We need to be apart to stay together. We need to be alone, both of us, to be together.

You need to get me alone.

For my own stupid, ugly, selfish reasons.

For my petty, shallow, overblown reasons. Supernova.

Self-worth: unreason: supernova.

Please be unreasonable. I am unreasonable. You're a child. I'm a child. I'm her only, perfect, stupid, worthless child who can't love.

Yes, Mom, I'm fine.

I'm lying.

Help me, please.

Know what I won't say.

Know me better.

Better, yes.

I want to be better.

I sit on the red futon you turned to ash. I lick the ash and this is the only thing I lick.

I lick my lips.

I lick an ice cube popsicle.

I freeze-dry myself onto any hard surface: preservation. This is what starvation feels like.

Please don't look at me like that.

Please don't touch me. I'll explode.

Objectified? Disrespected?

No.

   No.

This is what I want. I just want.

To cling to you.

To cling to your shoe.

What about the fish that die for rubber?

Follow your star to the dark horizon.

Redshift.

I just want all of you.

In the spring, I fly to Chicago because it's my turn. We've been apart for a month. My flight lands early, so I take my time getting to the baggage claim, and walk through the duty-free Hallmark store and Hudson News. I buy a Chicago snow globe for ten dollars even though I have no one to give it to. While I'm paying for it, I buy an extra pack of Orbit gum and a sugar-free Red Bull just because.

During our time apart, John registered for his summer class and we began planning what will happen in May. It's now early March. I'm surprised by his uncharacteristic show of initiative but I don't say so. I don't want to embarrass him.

In the car, I say that I want to go to the Adler Planetarium. John agrees, but instead we stay in and order Chinese food. I throw it up in the bathroom while John sits on the leather couch watching a documentary about the Zapatistas and drinking a case of Corona. I come out and stop by the bedroom, take two Hydroxycut from my purse, and drink them down with the broth from the vegetable soup without him noticing. I break open a fortune cookie but don't eat it. The fortune reads, *A journey of 1,000 miles begins with one step.* I show it to John. He doesn't care and he doesn't suspect anything.

We finish the documentary and he turns off the TV and tries to remove my shirt. At first I resist, but he tries again and I don't want him to feel rejected. We kiss and he goes down on me. I try to enjoy it.

I want you to be rough, I say.

How?

I don't want to fuck you. You have to make me.

We pause and he grabs my legs and pushes them down. He's drunk.

Make you what?

Make me fuck you.

Ow.

Make me fuck you.

I grab his hair and yank it.

Make me fuck you.

No.

Make. Me. Fuck. You.

Ow.

Hurt me. Get angry.

I hurt you, didn't I? Now you have to hurt me.

He goes to his room and brings out a basket from under his bed. There are nylon ropes inside.

This is the only way I can do it.

Fine.

Turn the fuck over.

He ties my hands and feet together. The ropes are soft and come untied with the slightest pressure. He has to keep stopping to retie them. This happens three times and then we give up and he tells me to pretend.

Don't be a fucking pussy. Make me hurt.

This is how I used to do it with Michele.

He holds my shoulders down and pretends to spit on my face. I picture Michele in my position. I picture his cock deep inside her.

I don't like that.

She hated it.

So do I.

Good. Shut up.

I'm serious.

I hold my wrists together because the ropes don't do it. I hold my feet together above the leather couch, so he can pretend they're bound there. I drift across the room and see him above me, see me lying still beneath him. He finishes on my ass and falls asleep. I stare at the dark TV.

Back in New York, I call him and lie.

I just threw up my food.

Why'd you do that?

I don't know. I just did.

He's quiet for a minute. Then he says, You said you wouldn't do that anymore.

Are you mad?

Yeah, I am.

Good. I want him to be mad.

It really hurts my feelings that you would lie to me, he says.

I didn't know how to tell you.

Are you doing it all the time?

Just sometimes.

Well, stop. Do you need to see a therapist?

I don't think so.

So you're going to stop?

Yeah.

Really?

Yeah.

Really?

Yeah. I'll stop.

You better. You know I'll tell your mother.

What the fuck?

I'm not putting up with it.

THE THIRD DREDGE-UP

THE RED GIANT DEPLETES THE HELIUM SUPPLY IN its core but continues fusing hydrogen into helium.

It builds in a shell around the core, and reignites in a flash, leading to a thermal pulse within the star.

Helium, carbon, and s-process products are brought to the surface, outweighing oxygen.

This is the third dredge-up.

John calls me three times a day in the month after he leaves to make sure I'm eating and keeping my food down. Sometimes I'm honest and sometimes I lie to him. When I'm honest, he's upset and I like this. I find being honest and lying equally useful. I text him a picture of a meal that I'm about to eat and then text him a picture of my empty plate half an hour later. Then I text him a picture of my mouth, open without food inside. This only seems to prove something. It's what he wants to see but he also wants me to call him later to tell him I've lied. He doesn't say so, but this message is as important as the first; it keeps us connected, circling.

We want to be concerned. It's what we have to talk about. It gives us something to do.

Someone to blame for our own behavior.

I really don't want to lie. I really do want to get better.

I'm afraid of this.

I want not to do this anymore. Not to think about what, when, how much, and what to do afterward.

I feel myself growing dimmer by the day.

I feel I'm growing cooler.

A white dwarf can cool to zero temperature but still have high energy.

I weigh myself once an hour when I'm home. Now that I'm eating for John, I can't help but eat all the time. I don't feel hunger when I feel it all the time. Now I know when I'm hungry — when I should be. I hate this.

I hate.

When I've eaten, I feel the food moving inside me. I buy groceries but don't digest them. They're gone within a day, down the toilet.

I can't stand the feeling of food. I feel it on my organs, feel it weighing me down.

I purge and then fear that I haven't purged it all and take pills to burn the remains.

I drink Red Bull like water.

I think of other ways to be empty.

He sends me articles about the dangers of constant purging but I find them motivational. He tells me he won't find me attractive without any teeth, but I think this won't happen to me.

I don't care if it does.

I also know it will happen but feel powerless to stop it.

Many times I kneel before the toilet not wanting to do what I finally do.

Many times I walk to Walgreens without deciding to do so. I find myself standing in the diet aisle and I don't know how I got there; it seems I was compelled.

I take Hydroxycut to the register and while I'm there, I buy *Star Magazine*. I don't know how it happens.

Miley Cyrus's Tiny Workout Clothes. Christina Aguilera Shows Off Sexy, Slim Figure on Music Video Shoot.

The 10 Ugliest Celebrities. The 15 Sexiest Sports Moments.

Ask Yourself These Questions: Know If It's Moods or Depression.

Win It! A Year's Supply of Pocket Protein.

I'm not dropping weight because I'm not always purging. I think about the zero-sum ways I abuse metabolism: I store more fat because I only starve sometimes. I eat more when I eat because I only starve sometimes.

I gain a couple of pounds because I can't purge constantly. I'm storing water because I'm dehydrated. I feel bloated all the time. I know that I smell bad.

I'm dizzy.

And I feel that my fate is inevitable.

I scratch my hands, my arms, I bite my nails.

I grind my teeth constantly.

An accretion disk is matter that is gravitationally drawn into the field of the black hole.

Quasars are regions surrounding black holes at the centers of young, active galaxies.

Angular momentum prevents the material from moving in a straight line into the region.

Instead, it spirals down into it.

I can't do it. I can't do this anymore.

At the end of the month, John calls me from jail. He's been arrested at a club for fighting with the bouncer, who kicked him out for sleeping at the bar. The bouncer wouldn't let him go back in to get Michele. John punched the bouncer in the face.

He kicked my head into the pavement. I have fifteen stitches.

I look up his mug shot. The wound starts at his left temple and travels to the middle of his cheek, winding around his cheekbone.

That's a horrible scar.

John, don't drink so much that you fall asleep at the bar. This scares me.

I wasn't drunk; I was tired.

Please don't do this anymore.

It's not a big deal. He laughs.

Michele thinks it's funny.

John lands at MacArthur airport the first week of May. I drive an hour and a half to meet him. I'm late, and by the time I arrive, he's been drinking at the concourse bar for thirty minutes. He's recently changed medications and sounds confused on the phone. He can't tell me where he is.

I walk in circles around the baggage claim and the drop-off, walk through the CNBC News gift shop and the Long Island Travelmart, and finally see him across the security checkpoint. I call his name but he doesn't hear me. I wave my arms but he doesn't see me. Finally, he answers his phone. We collect his bag from the rotating conveyor and start back toward my apartment.

It's just after sunset and stars are faintly visible on the horizon. We follow a featureless four-lane highway through acre after acre of grey parking lots and squat concrete strip malls with tattered awnings advertising pawn shops, check cashing places, Mexican restaurants, and used sporting goods stores. John takes my hand across the console and tells me about a documentary on the May '68 Paris uprising he thinks I should see. As he talks, he becomes more lucid, and I wonder if his prior confusion wasn't just the residual grogginess of an in-flight nap.

A wide pink scar wends its way down the left side of his face. I'll have to get used to its being there.

We begin to talk about what we should do this first night together. John jokingly tells me to stop at a strip club we pass, then together we decide to do it. I turn around and drive back half a mile. We're laughing as we pull inside. The sex shop next door has a mannequin in the window wearing a teddy shaped like Saturn's rings.

The club is sparsely attended. Four dancers and a handful of tired veteran patrons pass each other and keep walking toward opposite sides of the room. The red of the velvet booths folds into shadows on silver-speckled black carpet. The walls are covered in black vinyl peeling away at the corners. John orders us drinks: a Red Bull and vodka for me, and a Scotch for himself. He leaves the bar and two strippers take his place. The bartender fixes them drinks without them having to ask.

John sits next to me and hands me a blister pack.

What's this?

Ativan.

Is this your new prescription?

He nods.

I've never heard of it.

It's for anxiety. Take one.

No, I don't think so.

Trust me. They're not strong.

I turn the package over. The thin aluminum on the back pops open easily and a small yellow pill falls into my hand.

What's it going to do to me?

Relax you.

He pops another out for himself and washes it down.

We turn our attention to the stage. A bored stripper does basic tricks on the pole, looking nowhere in particular. Another checks her phone. A third dances for two businessmen sitting on the far side of the stage. They seem amused and talk to each other.

How long does it take to kick in?

Half an hour.

I walk around the room and see my students working together. Every time I pass my mentor's desk, I take a sip of my coffee. Last night, I told my only remaining friend that John and I are happy together. Whatever she may think she knows about him is not based in fact, I said. Remember that.

I left my friend at the table after dinner and purged silently in the bathroom.

I splashed my face with water and returned to the table. She suspected nothing.

I have even done it in restaurants with people in the stalls next to me, but not in a long time. I haven't needed to, as I don't go to restaurants anymore. This night was a rare exception.

My students are making visual aids of spiral-ins. Not messy enough, I say.

It's violent. They're gas. They won't hold together.

Picture one star eating another. Picture them both devastated.

Imagine bodies tearing through bodies.

I drag my hand in circles through a desk covered in plastic jewels. They scatter on the floor.

Like this.

Nothing is preserved but the cold, dead cores of the components. Sometimes not even those remain intact.

I want Styrofoam balls all over the floor. I want glitter everywhere. Broken pencils.

I want the floor covered in your partner's hair. Cut it off.

Here, use these craft scissors.

Don't be afraid to bleed a little.

A tooth will get you extra credit. A finger: automatic A+.

And if I find you in hard, little pieces at the end of the class, I'll make you dinner.

But not eat it.

I watch headlights approach and recede in the black distance from our ship in the strip club lot. John sleeps next to me, unaware that we've left the club. We've been asked to leave. They hurled us free.

Light pollution obscures the stars, but most things happen unseen. A spotlight on the neighboring building has us at its center.

John slept beneath the woman whose body turned rhythmic circles over his crotch. She curved and rolled. She rested her ass on his dick.

A body circled me, too.

I kept my hands on the sides of the chair. Her breasts brushed my cheek, soft and maternal. I closed my eyes and reentered the womb. A man's hand shook me awake.

You gotta leave.

Prolonged time spent in space will result in massive bone loss and musculoskeletal atrophy, severely inhibiting astronauts' long-term flight capabilities.

Take him with you.

Astronauts could sustain injuries reentering a gravitational field such as Earth's, or even stronger: that of Mars.

This is exacerbated by in-flight anorexia: a loss of appetite resultant of space's adverse affects on human metabolism.

I cannot control what my arms do. I feel that they don't belong to me.

(Sleep beneath her pressure.)

There are two mechanical forces: active and passive.

Wake up. I can't drive, John.

Wake up, John. Help me.

I reach for the keys but miss. My eyes bob open and shut. I put my head back.

One leg on one side and one on the other.

I can't see. Help me.

Wake up, John. Please.

He didn't know his body and hers came together. He didn't know when they separated. He breathed peacefully. Passively.

Can you drive?

She asked me what to do. I didn't know. I didn't care. I couldn't see. I was comfortable as I was.

Shut up.

I was comfortable there without body. I was gas floating in

the warm, dark walls. I turned to gas and floated away in the margins, moved like liquid mercury.

Had my own woman dancing. She was mine and I was nothing.

Open your eyes. Open them.

She was slim torso, long legs, full breasts, firm and encapsulating. She began as a nebula.

Open up. John, help me.

I slap my face. I slap the other side. Open my eyes. I'm awake. I slap myself again.

I'm awake. I'm awake. I'm awake. I'm awake.

John, I'm going to drive us home now. You need to help me.

I open the windows and shake him hard. I pull onto the road. I move in one direction.

Mom, please.

My arms are heavy and at the same time liquid.

I drive toward the silver gas of the city and the road's margins.

I can't do this. Mom, help me.

I shake and swerve and pull into another lot. I am always entering another lot. I am always arriving somewhere I didn't intend to be.

I put the seat back and the car spins around me. John wakes at the sudden movement. He's looking for what?

Where are we?

I don't know. Mercury.

John, I can't do this on my own.

My mentor finds me in the supply closet clutching coffee in one hand and a tissue in the other. Bits of tear-soaked tissue cling to my face. I am leaning on the pencil shelf.

What's wrong?

I have a thyroid disease.

My last night in Chicago, I helped John design our distro's

logo. We're calling ourselves Black Masque. We're selling zines, t-shirts, messenger bags, and the ideology of veganarchism.

And general Earth liberation.

We print the zines for free from the Internet and then we take our printouts to FedEx and make as many copies as we think we'll need — 25 or 50. We keep them on shelves in his apartment.

We buy solid t-shirts from American Apparel because American Apparel doesn't use sweatshops. We screenprint them with white ink if the shirts are black. If they're earth-tones, we use black ink. The ink is vegetable-based and nontoxic, and wasn't tested on animals. We ordered it online.

Our messenger bags will be sewn together from old jeans. I'll sew them myself, this winter, after the school year is over. Then, I'll mail them to John for screenprinting.

Most of our screenprints are the Black Masque logo: a free-standing figure holding a dog, wearing the signature mask. Other screenprints are anarchist slogans — some we found and some we devised:

Today's empire is tomorrow's ashes. We are the crisis.

People are not profits. Longer leashes / larger cages.

One direction: Insurrection. One solution: Revolution. This is my favorite.

In Arms! with a picture of a revolutionary hugging a rabbit.

We're planning to put the money we raise into a new project, one that's still crystallizing.

We wake at dawn in the parking lot of a Sealy mattress warehouse, hearing a tap at the window. A police officer asks us to step out of the car and show him identification. My keys are still in the ignition and my headlights have been on all night. A line of crusty drool has dried to the side of John's face. I motion for him to wipe it off but he doesn't see me.

I haven't eaten in over twenty-four hours and it's apparent

that we're both hung over. I lean against the car for balance. My head throbs. My hands shake. I'm faint. I feel like crying.

The officer leaves us standing with his partner by the trunk of the car and takes twenty or more minutes checking our records. When he comes back, John is rubbing the flesh between his eyes and looking around impatiently. He spits on the ground.

What brings you to New York?

Her.

What about you?

I go to Adelphi.

He hands our IDs back.

You all out drinking last night? Had a little too much?

We nod. He looks at John.

You got in trouble a few weeks ago, yeah? Assault? Drunk and Disorderly? Think maybe you should lay off for a while?

John keeps his eyes on the ground. The officer smiles at him and then walks to the front of the car and looks in the open door. He reaches inside and picks up something.

Ativan. You got a prescription for this?

Yep.

Can I see it?

It's in the backseat.

He waits while John opens the back door and rummages around in his duffel bag. John pulls out the box. The officer reads it closely and hands it back to him.

Why don't you go on home now.

He takes a long last look inside the car.

And maybe spend the next few nights there.

Greetings from the other side of the killing field.

We, Students for the Liberation of Animals, call for a non-violent revolution against all governments and organizations that aid or support the illegitimate terrorist state of the meat, dairy, and vivisection industries.

We are a decentralized group of autonomous cells. Any and all non-violent actions taken against these industries may be claimed as actions of Students for the Liberation of Animals.

From this day forward, we refuse to perpetuate or tolerate the killing of millions of innocent livestock, victims of vivisection, and our brothers and sisters of the sea. We will use any and all means of non-violent direct action including civil disobedience, the building of checkpoints at slaughterhouse and laboratory entrances, online insurrection, arson, vandalism, infiltration, and leafleting. We will no longer stand by and witness the needless slaughter of our brothers and sisters.

The time for revolution is now. We want the world to know that it is not the ALF, SHAC, ELF, Earth First!, or Students for the Liberation of Animals who are the terrorists but rather the capitalist state that forces us into roles as passive consumers dependent on factory farms and vivisection laboratories. Comrades, you grow fat, dumb, and indifferent on our couches and in our shopping malls while our brothers and sisters suffer and die at the hands of slaughterers and murderers in lab coats. Hear the cries of our brothers and sisters.

Animals and human animals alike have been forced into a position of desperate self-defense. Chickens endure painful debeakings and lifetimes of confinement in battery cages. They are forced to lay over twice as many eggs as is natural per year, molt and suffer constant abrasion against cages and pecking from other prisoners, only to be sent down the shaft and ground alive for Campbell's.

Cows are confined, constantly impregnated, milked dry, and fed a battery of hormones and antibiotics that harm them and their human consumers, suffer painful infections in their udders, and then are sent to slaughter when they're no longer useful for pouring milk over our Cocoa Puffs.

Monkeys and dogs cry from behind the bars of their prison cells, bleeding from the ears.

We are no longer deaf to their suffering cries.

We stand up in arms in their defense.

It's time for Americans of all backgrounds to protest and bring to justice those who oppress their brothers and sisters. Let us bring the struggle for the liberation of animals to the streets. Our numbers may be small, but we have passion and the dedication to use all our means to end this genocide.

We will bring freedom to our brothers and sisters by any means necessary.

We will end their suffering.

In solidarity,

Students for the Liberation of Animals

I've been in the university library since seven o'clock this morning. It's almost eleven o'clock at night. I have eaten two apples and five half-sticks of celery, a handful of almonds, and time. I have opened Adderall capsules and dropped them into water. I've crushed lines with my university ID and snorted them off the study desk. I've taken breaks to buy coffee from the food court, and have tried to take two ten-minute naps with my head on my arms, but failed. I hear everything around me. I'm alert and buzzing. My skin shakes on my flesh, I'm so cold.

I've chosen the coldest, brightest corner in which to confine myself.

I'm studying for a test of the evolution of cataclysmic variable stars. I glow faintly but burn no fuel. I accrete.

The smell of aging, moldy books in the cold reminds me of withered flesh, and of the passive drift of meteorites into orbit before they're burned away.

John has asked me to make the Facebook page for Students for the Liberation of Animals. He says that I use my words in a way he can't. I rewrote the manifesto.

Really, it's just that I'm not sleeping.

I didn't say that.

I didn't mean that. I'm sorry.

I'll do it.

I study for class and work on the Facebook page and go back to studying for class. I focus intensely but can't seem to focus for long: I go back and forth. I can't settle.

Every time I move my head in a certain way, the hunger gets

worse and I'm dizzy. I pull my hair so I don't feel my head throb. I bite my nails.

John will fly to Long Island next week. We're planning an action, the first we'll post on the SLA Facebook page. Of course, we'll include pictures. We'll say it was conducted by an independent cell that then contacted us.

Cataclysmic variables are binary systems in which the component stars seem to pulse.

They increase in brightness then rapidly drop back down to a state of quiescence.

I upload a user picture: a fist that clutches a freed rabbit aloft. I write, *We, Students for the Liberation of Animals, call for a revolution.*

I upload another user picture: a man in a black ski mask cradling a duck before a burning building. *Liberation by any means necessary!*

Cataclysmic variables require two stars: a white dwarf primary and a mass-transferring secondary. The white dwarf accretes matter from its companion.

I write a description: *Decentralized, independently operating units committed to liberating animals by any non-violent means. We act anonymously. We are your sons, your daughters, your soccer coaches, your neighbors. We are in your living room.*

If accretion exceeds the critical mass of the white dwarf, it will ignite runaway carbon fusion.

I drink the Adderall water. I snort a line.

I eat a baby carrot. I chew it longer than I need to. I chew another, but spit most of it into a napkin.

I tell myself I shouldn't have done that.

I make a gallery of suffering animals with captions: *Piglets are snatched from their mothers at only a few weeks old.*

When the sows are spent, they, too, are sent to slaughter.

The average life of a factory cow is five years. In nature, she can live as long as 20 years.

A suffering chimpanzee undergoing pharmaceutical tests at Huntingdon Life Sciences.

Huntingdon Life Sciences has repeatedly been found to cut corners and use unnecessarily cruel tactics.

An SLA member goes undercover at Huntingdon Life Sciences and lets these beagle puppies out of their cages for a few minutes of play.

The runaway carbon fusion triggers a Type-1a supernova explosion, completely destroying the white dwarf star.

Sponsored ads to the right of the page tell me about deals at Walgreens, Mac Cosmetics, United Airlines, and Forever 21.

I print the manifesto on a library printer. I stand and pack my laptop into my bag. I walk past the printers to the bathroom.

I look in the full-length mirror and pee and look in the full-length mirror again sideways, splash my face with water, and leave, watching myself in the mirror.

I walk past the information desk and make eye contact with the third undergraduate student I've seen here today. His face says that even he thinks I've been here too long.

Midterms, I say.

He nods.

I leave a stack of the manifesto on the table of university flyers near him. He doesn't notice.

I sit back down at the study desk and open my computer. I feel a wave of exhaustion overtake me in a cold, white swell. I rub my eyes. I focus on the Adderall buzz. I crack my fingers and cough. The exhaustion passes.

I make a note in Facebook and copy and paste the manifesto from John's email. I post it.

No one has liked the page, yet.

Wait until they see the first photos of SLA action. That'll get attention.

I fold my arms and put my head down.

They are also called eruptive variables.

Hi, Mom.

I'm okay. John flew in last night.

He's taking a class in the city. Starting next week.

Staying with me, of course.

I'm okay. Very tired.

Spring semester just ended.

I haven't seen it, yet, but all A's, I'm sure.

I got a job at Starbucks, starting this weekend.

I can walk there. Save on gas money.

I'm not going to drink the milk.

Not just health reasons anymore. That's still part of it.

I've been reading about...

Yes, ethical reasons. First.

I'm happy to send you some books.

I could maybe come home sometime in August. I don't know.

It depends on my schedule.

I miss you, too.

I'm tired.

I would tell you.

I'm just going through some stuff.

Mom, stop. I don't do drugs.

John doesn't work. It's complicated. He's never had to work.

His parents.

You can call me, too, you know.

Mom, what's the most important decision you've ever made?

I'm feeling lost. I feel like I haven't done anything important
with my life.

Graduation isn't enough.

I need to focus my energy.

I don't know what I care about.

I don't like myself.

I'm stuck in some kind of cycle.

I'm not happy.

I'm really depressed.
I don't know what to do.
I feel like I'm floating in space.
All alone.
Do you ever feel alone?
I'm scared.
I have to go.
I'll be fine.
I'll tell you.
Of course, Mom.
I always stay out of trouble.

At five o'clock, I walk to Starbucks and watch the sunrise while I prepare coffee. Venus hovers above the blue horizon and dawn breaks over the brushed metal, turning everything silver. I am light as fog.

I fill my first free cup of coffee just before I open the doors. My coworker arrives late but I don't say anything about it. She doesn't say anything to me. We move in circles around each other, getting ready for the morning rush. It took me twenty minutes to walk here and I was glad for the exercise, but by the time we open, I feel cranky.

I stay on the espresso machine while my coworker stays on the register. I enjoy the rhythmic, repetitive nature of the work. My hands move in automatic rhythms and I chat with customers across the counter. Many of them are lawyers on their way to the courthouse across the street. They flirt with me and I act charming. I drink my coffee between making lattes. I feel myself lifting off.

John packs me breakfast the nights before my opening shifts and leaves it in a bag on the kitchen counter. I pretend to forget them.

At eleven, he comes in and asks for a black coffee. The store is mostly empty now except for a cluster of writers in the corner and an elderly man who comes every day and reads J. Crew catalogues. John hands me the bag with my breakfast in it. He's upset.

You forgot this.

Thank you.

Did you eat something?

I look in the bag. There's a vegan granola bar and a banana inside, and a Tupperware of peanut butter.

Yeah.

What?

A banana.

He doesn't believe me but he doesn't say anything. Something else is on his mind. I sneak him a free coffee. He's brought his computer.

Are you going to stick around?

I want to finish reading something.

He takes his coffee to the window and sits in a red velvet chair with his computer on a small table. The lunch rush is light but a friend from class comes in and we talk for a minute before I introduce her to John. She's glad to meet him, but John is dismissive. He's too immersed in his reading to be interested. Although I don't know what it is, I explain that he's reading some difficult material. Still, she leaves confused. I text her later explaining it but she doesn't respond.

At the end of my shift, John is waiting for me outside, smoking a cigarette, staring at the courthouse.

Are you ready to go? I ask.

Yeah.

Are you okay?

No.

We walk in silence.

A group of radicals liberated a fur farm in Iowa, he says. They freed 1,200 foxes.

That sounds like a good thing.

Did you know that foxes are anally electrocuted? That's how fur farmers kill them.

That's awful.

We take the long way back toward my apartment, passing Chipotle, Qdoba, a combination Taco Bell/Pizza Hut, and a bar. John wants to stop and get a drink.

It's two thirty, I say.

He walks past me through the door.

I watched a video of a fox being electrocuted. He screamed like a human.

We sit at the bar and he orders himself a Boddington's Pub Ale, and orders me a Sierra Nevada.

I don't really want this.

I wanted to reach through the screen and stop them. I've never heard an animal make that sound before.

That night, John pushes me down. He cuffs my wrists together. He cuffs my ankles. The cuffs aren't real, but they work. He lays me on my side like a pig prepared for roasting.

He turns my head so I can't see him. I look at the dark corner.

I want you to come.

It's hard.

It shouldn't be hard if you love me. Come for me.

He pulses against me. Deep pulsations. I do what he says.

That's what I wanted.

The library stays open twenty-four hours during test weeks. I awake at one in the morning with my head on a stack of studies I've copied from scholarly journals. My computer screen has gone dark. The room is aglow with peripheral blur and my dry mouth tastes metallic. I drink from the Adderall water, but it's mostly spent. I stand and stretch and look around.

I am the only person here except for the student at the information desk who has also fallen asleep. Something moves by the copy machines: another student. He notices me but returns to his work. The distant hum of the air conditioner blends into the pulse of the copier and the silence between. I drink the rest of the water and walk a circle to the fountain and back, rub my face, and sit back down. I drink some more. My head is heavy with hunger.

I write: *Type-1a Supernovae Progenitors From Merging Binary White Dwarfs.* Underline it.

Traditionally, the scientific community has believed that mass accretion from a companion red giant pushed a white dwarf past the Chandrasekhar limit creating a standard-sized type-1a supernova explosion. This standard-sized explosion allowed for the use of type-1a supernovae as standard candles for measuring interstellar distances and the expansion rate of the Universe at different epochs. Indeed, it even allowed for the discovery of the dark energy instigating the acceleration of the Universe's expansion.

My chest expands and contracts. I turn the pages of a study. I set it aside and turn the pages of another study. My heartbeat skips and I return to the first. The white glow of the paper is blinding. I blink. The backs of my eyes feel hot.

I return to the first study and underline and make marginal notes on the first two pages. I do the same for the second. I stare at the space between the two for a long time without seeing anything. I realize I have not breathed for several seconds and take a deep breath.

However, recent studies throw doubt on our understanding of the causes of type-1a supernovae. Intercontinental analysis of 23 type-1a supernovae shows them exploding with different luminosities, suggesting that up to 75 percent likely originate, not with single degenerates accreting matter from main-sequence companions, but from merging double degenerates.

John calls me and the sound of my phone makes me jump. He has not taken his pills. Otherwise, he'd be asleep.

I'm in the library. I can't talk.

I have new information, he says.

I'll call you when I leave. Why aren't you sleeping?

I've stopped taking my medication. There's too much to do.
I have a paper due at eight. Let me finish and call you after.
I've made a list of supplies.
Just send me everything. I'll find what we need.
Pay cash, he says.

I lie on the grass of the quad and feel the distance between my class and me. The difference between my class and me is vast. I don't belong in a class.

I feel I don't belong anywhere. I feel I don't belong. I feel estranged from my body. It weighs me down. The best is to do away with it: be light.

Be free.

Shine without physicality.

I see myself as I am on the grass. I see myself as someone sees me. I see I am the grass.

Feminine, happy, successful, confident, alluring, intelligent: the dark body that draws your gaze magnetically toward it.

Kelly Rowland Admits She Was Jealous of Beyoncé. I spin. The grass is cold, wet flesh.

I turn; draw away. I find this disgusting.

I find myself disgusting.

My body is disgusting.

A wreck.

5 Instagram Tips Everyone Needs To Follow According to The #RichKids of Beverly Hills.

Please don't touch me, Earth. I'll wreck you.

When animals feel they're backed into a corner.

Brooke Burke-Charvet on That Sexy Gas Pumping Photo: "It Could Have Been Bad."

I rise and flow to the concrete monolith, enter through the double-doors, pace the halls.

Is This Demi's Best Hair?

I turn in celestial *communiqués* for a living to my professors: manifesto.

Please approve of the work I do. That's all I ask.

To be a good worker or to do without.

Arms, legs.

Or to finally stand alone.

In June, my coworker invites me out for drinks after our shift. My birthday has just passed and she buys me a Bacardi and Diet, and a Smirnoff and tonic for herself. She tells me she moved to New York from Oregon with her girlfriend and their dog. Her girlfriend's parents didn't approve of her being a lesbian and after months of suffering demonization from her mother, they thought it best to leave. My coworker is majoring in biology with a minor in poetry. When she can, she takes her dog to Jones Beach.

She's only working at Starbucks because they have health insurance and stock options, and plans to leave if she gets into grad school at Harvard or MIT, where she's currently applying.

John joins us halfway through our first drinks and orders a Dewar's on the rocks. He's had a few beers already, at home, and I can picture the cluster of bottles left by the trashcan. My coworker tells me how she misses her parents' farm.

What kind of farm was it? I ask.

A dairy farm.

Gross, John says.

My coworker looks at me.

We're vegan, I explain.

Oh, sorry. I didn't realize. I grew up on a farm, I could never be vegan.

Did your father send a lot of cows to slaughter when they stopped giving milk? John asks.

Excuse me?

Did you feel bad separating the calves from their mothers

when they were only a few days old? Did they scream until their throats bled?

I don't understand.

Do you miss bearing witness to the millions of tons of greenhouse gases cattle fart into our atmosphere every year?

I'm going to go.

Please don't, I say.

I don't know what his deal is. I didn't mean to offend you.

You didn't.

My deal is that I don't believe in enslaving non-human animals and damaging the environment so that you can butter the bread on your grilled cheese sandwich.

Okay, I'm leaving.

John, stop, I say.

He looks at me.

No, I'll go. You two have fun.

John leaves. We sit in silence.

I'm sorry. I should probably go talk to him.

Happy birthday.

Write this down.

— In the case of a double-degenerate explosion, nothing of either white dwarf will remain.

Stand. Go to your partner. Don't wait.

I walk in a circle around the room. I look into the face of each student. I have eaten nothing since the day before yesterday evening. I carry a leaking black Starbucks Venti coffee in my hand because last night I read that the Grande has four times the amount of caffeine as a Red Bull, so I thought I'd do better.

Remember this:

— The two stars orbit tightly. Some say they're magnetic.

Take your partner's hands. Orbit so tightly, there is nothing between you. Make sure your breath is foul and she smells it.

– They will orbit so tightly, they are not even aware of the force that binds them.

Squeeze your partner's hands until both of you are numb.

– There is no telling who leads and who follows. Neither. It's as if they're compelled.

Look your partner in the eye. Say *I love you*. Lie if you have to. Don't even know why.

– They orbit until they come close enough to collide.

Bash your partner in the head.

Do it hard. There should be nothing left.

Grind his brains into the carpet.

That's right, let it out. Use your heel. Use your nails.

Remember that time he spit on you? Now's your chance to get back at him.

Really let him feel it. Be cruel. Merciless. Petty.

Now tell him you love him.

Tell him you'll die if he leaves you.

After school, I sit in my car in the parking lot. I smoke a cigarette even though that's illegal within 1,000 feet of a school. I leave the windows closed. I listen to but don't hear the static coming from my speakers on B-103. I bite all my fingernails off one after the other but don't realize it until I'm done.

My mentor's crotch appears in the passenger window, in my periphery. His khaki Dockers bunch like he has a short, flaccid dick. I roll the window down.

His face appears at crotch-level.

Want to talk?

Not really.

Can we talk anyway?

I unlock the doors and he climbs inside. He moves the seat back and adjusts his pants. He closes the door.

You don't have a thyroid disease.

I keep my eyes on the steering wheel. I don't say anything.

I don't know what's going on with you, but whatever it is, I think you need to see a doctor. That's just my opinion, but I hope you know that I wouldn't have shared it if I didn't think you needed to hear it.

I appreciate your concern.

Do you really?

I drag the rest of my cigarette down to the filter and open the window and toss it out. I wave my hand back and forth in front of my face, clearing the smoke.

Listen, I don't really want to say this, but I don't think you should come back to the school until you deal with whatever this is. I don't know if it's drugs or whatever—

It's not drugs.

Or whatever it is. It's destructive, and I think you need help. You're a great teacher, but some of the kids have noticed. I can't have that in my classroom, and you know that. I can put you in touch with—

No, thank you.

Well... I guess that's all, then.

I feel him looking at me as I start the car and light another cigarette. He gets out and shuts the door, and leans down in the window.

You can call me anytime.

John oversleeps his flight at the end of August. We pull into the airport parking lot and see it taking off. The next flight to Chicago doesn't leave until tomorrow, unless he wants to buy a new ticket from a different airline. Unless his parents want to buy him another ticket.

I shook and shook him. I called his name and left and came back and shook him some more. I begged. The sun rose.

I lifted his head from the sheets.

We watch the plane until it disappears, then leave the airport and come back the next morning, early. We pass Cadillac,

Hummer, and Lexus dealerships, Baptist and Catholic churches, bail bondsmen, Best Buy and Home Depot, all of them grey.

We have to be sad about his leaving all over again. I'm upset. John is sadder than he was yesterday.

What's Behind Bieber's Bad Behavior?

I'm crying but I'm not sure why. It's not for John.

Can you please not be mad at me? he says.

I'm not mad.

I won't see you for a month, at least.

I'm not mad.

If you say so.

Something is wrong with me.

He opens his messenger bag and pulls out a notebook.

I didn't know you kept a notebook.

I want to show you something.

All of the pages are covered in microscopically small writing. He's left no white space at all. In the corners of some, he's drawn little pen-and-ink sketches. He turns to a page near the back.

I found this.

He hands me a glossy photograph he's torn out of a magazine. The edges are rough. He had a hard time tearing it cleanly. In it, a mid-sized house is nestled perfectly into the upper branches of a mature oak. The forest around the house is darkening but a warm yellow glow lights up the windows.

This is beautiful.

I want to live there with you.

Are you buying a tree house?

Not now, someday. When we've done everything in life that we want to do. This is the world I want to live in.

A woman's silhouette is visible in a floor-to-ceiling kitchen window. She seems to be looking down at the photographer. I squint, trying to make out her expression, but it's hidden in shadow.

He takes the picture back.

Wait, can I keep it?

Really?

Yeah. I want it.

I put it in my glove compartment.

You're going to miss your flight.

We walk across the bleached parking lot to the small steel building. Its windows reflect the late morning sun like balls of fire.

I hand John his suitcase. He sets it between us, and kisses me over it.

I don't want to wait long to see you.

You won't. We'll find a way.

    Be good.

I'm always good.

He takes off.

Like a boat through water, moving celestial objects make ripples in the curvature of space-time.

I'm late for my Starbucks shift. There's no reason; I just didn't arrive on time. I'm in a fog. I haven't slept since John left. I feel that I'm entering a new phase of sickness. I've lost interest in sleep altogether; at four a.m., I realize it's four a.m. Still, I'm not tired.

I'm exhausted.

Each night, I stay on the Internet until I feel the paper-thin light of dawn fingering its way through the curtains. I read stories about stars. I read reviews of diet pills. I scroll through endless Tumblr pages of women thinner than I am. Endless Instagram pages. Google image searches. I look at them and look at my body and look at them and get up and look in the mirror. I walk toward the mirror and away. I turn around.

I make a revolution.

I twist into one position after another. I lie on the floor and stretch. I make curves, stand, and turn.

Truth is a permanent revolution.

I'm covered in bruises.

My boss is here. We go about the day as usual. Every hour, I make a new carafe. I clean the bathroom. I am always on the schedule to do this. I unload shipments of Chicken BLT Salad Sandwiches, Turkey Havarti Sandwiches, Chonga Bagels, 8-Grain Rolls, Almond Cookies, Apple Fritters, Blueberry Oat Bars and Scones.

I talk to the regular customers. They like me but seem not to be as exuberant today.

I drink as many free cups of coffee as I want, which is six, so far.

I take frequent cigarette breaks. In the August heat, I sweat through my requisite white collared shirt. My skin is moist and I wipe off the sweat with my apron, then drop it into my lap.

I blow smoke into its folds.

John texts me.

Do we have everything we need?

I have it all. I'm ready.

This is going to be big.

Truth is in constant revision; truth can only approximate reality. I say this like a mantra.

Truth is a vision — say it.

I don't believe that John believes.

As I'm putting my apron back on, my boss comes outside.

Leave the apron inside when you smoke.

I wasn't wearing it.

You're blowing smoke on it.

I wasn't.

You were. I just watched you through the window.

He lets the door close behind him and crosses his arms. I've never liked my boss.

I was aiming it that way, I say.

Would you agree that this is not working out?

Would I agree?

You working here.

Oh, I knew what you meant.

He sits down at a plastic table and invites me to join him. Two of our regular customers walk past us. They wave. I wave back.

People have told me you're giving free coffee to customers.

Just my boyfriend, one time.

They say you've been doing it a lot.

Not true.

Regardless, one time is too much.

I wipe the sweat from my face with the end of my apron. Inside, my coworkers talk and look at us.

Enough to fire someone?

There are other things, he says.

Like what?

It's probably best not to say. I think you know, anyway.

Hunger burns and rises in my chest.

Are you firing me?

I think it's probably best.

I'm on fire.

I look at the courthouse. Men and women in suits step lightly as needles into its marble entrance.

Do you know that Starbucks uses almost a million gallons of milk every year? I say.

I did not know that.

Fuck you. Did you know that the Cinnamon Chip Scone has more calories in it than a Quarter Pounder With Cheese?

He looks away.

That's fucking disgusting, I say. You self-righteous prick. You're a terrorist who works at a fast food restaurant.

I stand and take off my apron and throw it in his face.

Have fun cleaning the bathroom, shithead.

Two possible scenarios exist for the expulsion of a star from a binary system.

In the first, a member of the system explodes in a supernova, kicking the other member out.

In the second, a binary system collides with a third star, changing the stars' velocities.

This change in velocity causes a member to gather energy and escape as a runaway.

Its matter points back to its former association. We can trace its origin.

It's been less than a month. John calls me fifteen minutes before his flight is supposed to leave Chicago to tell me he's not on the plane. I'm sitting on the hood of my car in the Walgreens parking lot, reading a *Star Magazine*. My trunk is full of combustibles, wire cutters, black clothing, bleach.

Dog is dead, he says.

No.

She chewed through my Ativan. I don't know how she found it.

John, I'm so sorry. Jesus, fuck. At least you know she didn't suffer.

I thought I left it in the cabinet. She puked all over the bed.

I'm so sorry.

I listen to him cry for a long time. Two girls cross the parking lot carrying bottles of Coke and bags of Skittles. They climb into a red Jaguar and the radio comes on at full volume with the engine, shaking the air.

John's still crying.

Where is she now?

She's here. I just found her.

Just now?

Just now, he says.

Like, how long ago?

Ten minutes.

Burn.

I don't get it. You were supposed to be at the airport hours ago. Were you sleeping before then?

He doesn't answer. I feel angry. I listen to him cry. I try to feel pity but I can't.

You're an animal. I'm an animal.

I can't do this, I say.

Yes, you can. Show me you're with me. He blows his nose.

You lied.

About what?

Loving me.

Dog is dead.

You killed her.

Excuse me?

Murderer.

That's not fair.

Burn. We're through.

What do you mean?

Fuck you.

Are you breaking up with me?

This is over.

Can't this wait?

I don't love you.

My dog is dead. I doubt your commitment.

You should. I'm alone and I like it.

You're crazy.

You deserve what you've done.

You don't know me.

Who are you? I can't be with a dog killer. She needed you and you killed her.

You deserve to be alone. You're fucked.

Don't call me anymore. I don't know you.

I can't believe this.

   This will blow up in your face.

It already has.

Hi, Mom.

Can I talk to you for a minute?

I got my grades. They're not as good as last semester's.

I've been going through some personal things.

I've ascended.

I don't have an appetite. Sleep. Or friends.

I'm very lonely.

I'm stuck in this terrible cycle.

It seems everyone has disappeared. They don't answer. I stay up all night on the Internet.

I'm confused.

I'm endlessly scrolling, scrolling.

I can't leave the house. I'm insane.

I read books on animal liberation. I feel they're about me. I feel it's me, Mom.

I haven't been okay.

I need you. Help me.

Please help.

I want you to be proud.

There's something else.

We broke up.

John lies. He only cares about himself.

I've been used.

Not by him. In general.

Mom, listen. I want to say I love you.

Do you believe me?

Please believe me.

I'm cold.

I'm lost.

I'm afraid.

And angry.

Desperate.

All the time. I've come unbound. I'm fading away.

I don't know what's going to happen.

I'm burning out.

You make time for what you think is important. Didn't you say that?

We've forgotten what's important. We have no sense of balance. No value.

I know what I have to do, Mom.

I'm making sense for the first time. Trust me.

Anything can happen but I know it's related to light.

I really do.

I'm going to make you proud.

And I love you.

I'm suffering.

I'm done.

I'm done suffering.

But about the tree house?

I'm alone, I act alone. Anonymous.

I've had nothing to eat for three days. I shake. I drink coffee. I feel that my body is crystallizing. I feel it beginning at the center. A stellar wind flows from my atmosphere, shedding matter in ionized gas. I'm charged. I leave trails of myself behind me. My path is neutral. My movement is relative.

It was named after the Beatles song, "Lucy in the Sky With Diamonds."

It is only a lattice.

A lattice wraps around his back porch, painted white, a swing-set, a family, barbecues on the patio, mornings at the table.

Morning is continuous.

I crouch in the bushes. I crawl between the bushes and the wall, in black, unseen, related to darkness. Is it empty?

Vacant?

I'm gas.

He has it coming.

I crawl beneath the porch, beneath the back, leave paper trails behind me.

I doubt his commitment.

I pace the halls of the school. I got here early. My mentor will see me. I'm very indifferent. Extremely. And I smell like gasoline.

I can be your daughter with purpose. I'm purpose. Nonviolent. Who was injured?

The house should be vacant. The task is inevitable. I'm sharp and fill space. I light the paper with other lit paper and throw it into shadows.

The dean of the college is coming.

Were you asked not to stay? Do you agree?

Do I?

I agree we're sentient beings. I agree we're not the terrorists.

Huntingdon Life Sciences Vivisector Victim of Arson.

I'm confused.

Talk in circles on the phone. Write this down.

We saw each other's bodies. I stood in the corner of the yard and he stood in the center. He named me.

What are you doing here?

Fading.

Cruelty of Laboratory Practices Exposed.

What are you doing? I have a family.

I told you to get them out. You've failed.

Eco-Terrorist.

Fat and indifferent.

I told you to leave hours ago. You didn't listen. Now there's fear.

Stand for our brothers and sisters. In arms.

Fill and empty.

Now you're afraid, aren't you? Now you're backed into a corner. Now you bite the hand.

Crystallization begins in the center.

What are you saying?

Hidden Cameras.

Director Steps Down. Raging Fire. Targets Loose.

Jagged and dense.

I'm clear.

Luminous.

Still afraid.

I've had two cups of coffee and a Red Bull, two grapes and two cups of green tea. Two Adderall crushed in water.

Eaten time.

On fire.

Saved his family.

Get out before your house is in flames.

I called from the Walgreens parking lot, from the pay phone on the corner.

Runaway Arsonist.

Possible Witness.

I moved the scale to the hallway: 85. I have Zantrex-3, gum and ice. I have fingers. Numb. Sweat in circles.

Licking upward.

I acted alone in the dark dressed in black, invisible like always.

Warning to All Involved.

He came outside as I finished and watched from the shadows.

He saw I was small, female.

Recessing like us all.

Adelphi's counseling center can help.

I'm not teaching.

Stomach burns and rises in the chest. Head is heavy.

I'm expanding.

I ran away into darkness, looking back at his house lit up from beneath.

Still expanding.

The floor is cool. I sweat and breathe.

All that is left is a remnant.

I roll.

I'm old.

I rise.

Burn out.

On fire.

I walk down the hall to the bathroom. I'm nothing but an echo. I'm alone.

When can I stop? Were there children?

Victim's Family Says They're Well After Trauma.

Police Hunt for Arsonist.

We, Students for the Liberation of Animals.

We, Student Animals.

I'm a cunt.

Liberation by any means.

Stand up for your sisters and brothers.

Stand Up.

How are my thighs?

If he didn't leave, it's his fault, not mine.

I rest my head on the seat.

My abdomen hardening. Burns when I breathe.

Antimatter.

Locks Glued.

Torn Down.

Back of the class.

Axes.

My mentor is here.

Thanks for coming. Sit.

I'm fine standing.

Or I'm burning calories. Or I bend at the knees. Tunnel vision.

I heard them scream in the darkness.

Activists Stand Against Cruelty.
I'm afraid. He was afraid.
You have what it takes.
Your students need you.
I lean on the desk.
You've something authentic.
Like fire?
Arson Claimed as Action of Eco-Terrorist Cell.
I fall to my knees.
I'm faint.
You exhibit these principles.
I'm throwing up blood.
I'm reeling. I'm reeling.
I'm reeling.
I shine.

Acknowledgements

Many, many people helped this book reach you, reader. My deepest, most heartfelt thanks to my mom and dad, who taught me that empathy and health are important above all else. To my family, whose constant love and support keep me sane. To my first reader, David Formentin, who meets me in our passion for storytelling.

I'm infinitely grateful for the guidance of Adriann Ranta and the tireless, inspiring work of Eric and Eliza Obenauf. I owe special thanks to Adjua Greaves, *Binary Star*'s second reader and first copy-editor, and to Keith and Lucy Bailey, who opened up a home for me for a month while I wrote this.

Thank you, Sarah McNally, and the brilliant, dedicated booksellers of McNally Jackson for all that you taught me, and continue to teach me, which I could never hope to summarize. And thank you, Betsy Sussler, and the staff of *BOMB Magazine*, for giving my writing a place to grow so early in its life—and for everything you've done and continue to do for artists.

Of course, I owe a great debt to my instructors at The New School for their time and expertise: Ann Hood, Shelley Jackson, Helen Schulman, Dale Peck, Jonathan Dee, and John Reed, who has also been a great mentor and friend to me. Justin Taylor and Susan Shapiro have also been wonderful mentors and friends.

My fellow writers, the most profound thanks to you for sharing your work with me, and for your ceaseless reading and rereading, draft after draft: Rachel Hurn, Whitney Wimbish, Amanda Harris, Carly Dashiell, and Ken Derry.

And to all who have struggled and continue to struggle with food: keep fighting. There is a world for you.

CRYSTAL EATERS
A NOVEL BY SHANE JONES

"A powerful narrative that touches on the value of every human life, with a lyrical voice and layers of imagery and epiphany." —*BuzzFeed*

"[Jones is] something of a millennial Richard Brautigan." —*Nylon*

A QUESTIONABLE SHAPE
A NOVEL BY BENNETT SIMS

"[*A Questionable Shape*] is more than just a novel. It is literature. It is life." —*The Millions*

"Presents the yang to the yin of Whitehead's *Zone One*, with chess games, a dinner invitation, and even a romantic excursion." —*The Daily Beast*

MADE TO BREAK
A NOVEL BY D. FOY

"With influences that range from Jack Kerouac to Tom Waits and a prose that possesses a fast, strange, perennially changing rhythm that's somewhat akin to some of John Coltrane's wildest compositions." —*HTML Giant*

RADIO IRIS
A NOVEL BY ANNE-MARIE KINNEY

"Kinney is a Southern California Camus." —*Los Angeles Magazine*

"[*Radio Iris*] has a dramatic otherworldly payoff that is unexpected and triumphant." —*New York Times Book Review*, Editors' Choice

THE ORANGE EATS CREEPS
A NOVEL BY GRACE KRILANOVICH
* National Book Foundation 2010 '5 Under 35' Selection.
* *NPR* Best Books of 2010.
* *The Believer* Book Award Finalist.

"Krilanovich's work will make you believe that new ways of storytelling are still emerging from the margins." —*NPR*

ANCIENT OCEANS OF CENTRAL KENTUCKY
A NOVEL BY DAVID CONNERLEY NAHM

"Wonderful... Remarkable... it's impossible to stop reading until you've gone through each beautiful line, a beauty that infuses the whole novel, even in its darkest moments."
—NPR

HOW TO GET INTO THE TWIN PALMS
A NOVEL BY KAROLINA WACLAWIAK

"One of my favorite books this year." —*The Rumpus*

"Waclawiak's novel reinvents the immigration story."
—*New York Times Book Review*, Editors' Choice

THE CAVE MAN
A NOVEL BY XIAODA XIAO

* *WOSU* (NPR member station) Favorite Book of 2009.

"As a parable of modern China, [*The Cave Man*] is chilling."
—*Boston Globe*

THE PEOPLE WHO WATCHED HER PASS BY
A NOVEL BY SCOTT BRADFIELD

"Challenging [and] original... A billowy adventure of a book. In a book that supplies few answers, Bradfield's lavish eloquence is the presiding constant." —*New York Times Book Review*

"Brave and unforgettable. Scott Bradfield creates a country for the reader to wander through, holding Sal's hand, assuming goodness."
—*Los Angeles Times*

THE DROP EDGE OF YONDER
A NOVEL BY RUDOLPH WURLITZER

* *Time Out New York*'s Best Book of 2008.
* *ForeWord* Magazine 2008 Gold Medal in Literary Fiction.
"A picaresque American *Book of the Dead*... in the tradition of Thomas Pynchon, Joseph Heller, Kurt Vonnegut, and Terry Southern." —*Los Angeles Times*

Part-thriller, part-nightmarish examination of the widening gap between originality and technology, told with remarkable precision. Haunting and engaging, *The Removals* imagines where we go from here.

Coming 2016
Written by Nicholas Rombes
Directed by Grace Krilanovich

On an overcast Wednesday afternoon, Patrick N. Allen took his own life. He is survived by his father, Patrick, Sr.; his step-mother, Patricia; his step-sister, Patty; and his twin brother, Seth.

Coming 2015
Written & Directed by Eric Obenauf